GIL'S GRIMOIRE:
THE ZEROS AND
THE SEASON OF THE WITCH

BY ERIC BONKOWSKI

COPYRIGHT

DEDICATION & GRATITUDE

For John Rorer and Erin McMonigle, my #1 and #2
fans, respectively. Thank you for your loyal
friendship and unending support.

And for Dean. Thank you for your
friendship and generosity.

Oh, and for Kathleen. Of course.

ALSO BY THE AUTHOR:

Two Zeros and The Library of Doom!

The Zeros and The Man Who Could Not Die

The Zeros and The Season of The Witch

The Zeros and The Empirical Evidence of Stars
(forthcoming)

Brick Brannigan is Knee-Deep in Peril!

Brick Brannigan is Buried Alive in the Faroe Islands!
(forthcoming)

A NOTE TO THE READER:

Be sure to read the sample chapter at the end of the book from the next full-lenght novel of the Zeros, *The Zeros and The Empirical Evidence of Stars*, available soon from Penny Dreadful Publications. Visit http://www.gilsgrimoire.com for more information.

GIL'S GRIMOIRE:

THE ZEROS AND THE SEASON OF THE WITCH

"This is no longer a vacation. It's a quest."

- Clark W. Griswold

CHAPTER 1. A SUNNY DAY

You'd expect a story like this to begin a few days prior to Halloween and culminate with an extraordinary battle to the death on All Hallow's Eve itself—perhaps with the very fate of the world at stake.

Alas, my friend, you would be wrong.

Instead, let's begin in June, and a scorching, sunny day in June, at that. I had a radio beside me, running on batteries, telling the tale of another impending Phillies loss to the tune of static hiss and white noise. The volume was cranked, but I could barely hear it over the crash of the waves and children's laughter. I took a sip of a cold Yuengling and wiped the sweat from my brow. Somewhere nearby, the mercury was closing in on 100°.

Beer, baseball, and sand. Where else would I be but knee-deep in vacation at the beach? Rehoboth Beach, Delaware, to be exact. A short two-hour hop, skip, and jump from our hometown digs in Philadelphia. (And Delaware beaches > Jersey shore, for the record. Sorry).

"I certainly do not understand this," Finch said. "I was under the mistaken impression that once central air conditioning became the norm, people would not relish the opportunity to sweat in public as much as they seemed to."

"It's vacation, man," I said, taking another sip. "Enjoy it."

"Were you even alive prior to the advent of air conditioning?" he asked with a frown. Any passing stranger may find this question surprising given the fact that Finch appeared to be no more than a twenty-something art student. In actuality, he was a few hundred year-old guy cursed to live forever in the body of a twenty-something art student. I'd learned over the past few months that appearances could certainly be deceiving.

"Well... not so much," I said.

"As I expected," Finch said, licked a finger, and turned a page in a massive hardbound book he cradled in his lap. "Young people," he mumbled. "Who knows." He sat beneath a broad umbrella, completely bathed in shadow. Despite the nigh-triple digit temperatures, he was dressed in long pants, a long sleeve shirt, and shoes–all black.

"What are you reading?"

"Kierkegaard," he said. "You?"

"*Sports Illustrated.*"

"I must say, I admire the way you choose to challenge yourself, Dylan, even when on holiday. That is certainly stimulating material."

"No need to get grouchy, Finch," I said.

He sighed and closed his book. "You are right. I apologize. I just... well, I find this heat intolerable."

"Why not put on some shorts, Gramps?"

I looked up to see my boss, Gil, stumble towards our oasis among a sea of sunblock-lathered bodies, and I could not help but smile.

Gil Abercrombie, the benefactor, heart, and soul of our band of do-gooders known as *The Zeros*. You wouldn't be able to tell by the fiery sunburns, farmer's tan-lines, unkempt salt and pepper hair, Hawaiian-printed board shorts, or lion-shaped kite in hand that he was old enough to join the AARP.

Finch sighed. "Boss, I choose not to wear shorts because the sun is bad for my complexion."

"Just lather up!" Gil said with a characteristic smile as he tossed Finch an industrial-sized bottle of suntan lotion. "You're not havin' any fun tucked away under the umbrella reading *War and Peace* or whatever! Let's go in the ocean! Let's play sharks and minnows! Hell, Dottie even packed my boogie board."

Dottie–our trusty assistant and office adminis-trator–had actually packed Gil a whole bag of beach toys. Any passerby would probably think we had a child with us somewhere considering the assortment of shovels, buckets, sand molds, inflatable balls, rafts, and toy trucks that littered the sand around our um-brella. Gil had abandoned all when he'd grown jealous of a young boy's kite and purchased one of his own.

"Quite tempting," Finch said. "But no, thank you."

"How 'bout you, big man?" Gil asked, turning to me. "Beach golf? Sand darts? Bocce ball? Wanna build a sand castle?"

"How about volleyball?" I asked, turning my attention to the smattering of people milling around a makeshift sand court near the boardwalk. "How's your serve?"

"Oh, no, no, no, no," he said, recoiling as if I'd just suggested we get together to do our taxes. "I don't do the whole 'physical exertion' bit–unless it's sand darts. Or bocce ball. Or beach golf. And some-times building a sand castle, I guess. But not volley-ball, no. To quote Austin Powers: it's just not my bag, baby."

Finch sighed again. "All right, then why not show our new partner your not unimpressive skills in the realm of aerial ballet?"

Gil twitched his mustache from side to side. After a moment, he said, "*Huh*?"

"The kite," Finch said, opening his book once again. "Why not show Dylan how to fly the kite?"

"That's a *great* idea!" Gil said, his beet-red face lighting up. "What say you, big man?"

"It's... uh, not on the absolute top of my list," I admitted, eyeing the volleyball court once more as a game began.

Gil groaned. "Ugh, here I am at the beach, a beautiful day, and it turns out I'm with two complete fuddy-duddies. Would you rather be back at the off-ice, up to your big, bald head in paperwork?"

"Well, no–"

"Then come on!"

He kicked sand in my direction before turning and stumbling through a maze of chairs and sun-bathers towards a less-crowded section of beach. I stood resignedly and looked at Finch.

"You couldn't have just let me relax?"

He looked up at me and smiled a far-too-satisfied smile. "You know Boss," he said. "If someone is not keeping him entertained, it is terribly difficult to get any reading done."

"My turn?"

Finch smiled. "Seeing as you made me *humiliate* myself last night so you could go to the bar and watch that sporting event—"

"Putt-putt golf is not *humiliation*, Finch—"

"Of course it's humiliation! Those clubs are so damnably short, no one can be expected to exercise proper posture or technique with a *plastic* child-sized golf club." He shook his head, disturbed at even the memory. "So you can consider this your penance, my friend."

"All right, all right. I guess that's fair."

"Come on, Dylan!" I heard the Boss shout from down the beach. I turned and saw him waving ecstatically for me to join him.

"Fair, indeed," Finch said, going back to his reading. "Now we are even."

I turned and walked through the crowds, careful not to kick sand on any sleeping babies as I pulled my Flyers hat low to keep the sun out of my eyes. The sun was starting to sink, and dinner-time was not far off, so beach-goers had finally begun packing up, vacating just enough room to make kite-flying a possibility.

Gil stood a few hundred yards down the beach next to a young kid who had a kite similar to his. The boy looked rather dejected, his kite laying nose-down in the sand while Gil's hung far above, kite string taut in the strong ocean wind. I was too far away to hear anything, but I could see Gil speaking and gesturing, trying to help the kid get his kite airborne.

"–but if I wasn't holding this kite here, kiddo, I'd be your kite buddy. It's way easier to get kites in the air if you've got a kite buddy."

"How did you get yours up, mister?"

"Well, not to brag or nothin', but I'm real good, see?"

"Yeah."

"I'll help you though, man, don't you worry."

"Okay."

"My kite buddy will be here momentarily... There he is now!"

I looked down at the withered dragon kite on the ground in front of Gil's young friend, a freckled red head. "Having some problems, big guy?"

"I can't get my kite into the air."

"What's your name?"

"Jim."

"Hi, Jim. My name's Dylan. And this is Gil. I swear, we're not creepy."

Jim shrugged. "Okay."

"How did you get that up in the air, Boss?" I asked, turning to Gil.

"I told you, man, I'm good at this. Been doin' it for years, really."

"All right, but it doesn't help with this little problem," I said, gesturing at Jim's felled dragon.

"Yeah, true enough." He chewed his lip for a minute and squinted his eyes in thought, perhaps deciding if young Jim was worth interrupting his kite flying. Finally, he said, "Hold this," and handed me his kite reel.

"All right, Jimmy, here we go. You ready?"

Gil's new friend nodded his head.

"Hold the reel and feed some line out." The young boy complied slowly as Gil nodded his head. "Good, good. A little more." The Boss knelt and picked up the kite. "Keep feeding it and I'm going to take a few steps back, okay?"

Slowly, the kite line between Gil and Jim began to grow. When Gil was almost fifty feet away, he began to raise his arms.

"You gonna start running now?" I called to him. "I'd like to see that."

"You don't need to run, big man! Don't give the kid bad ideas."

"You ain't gettin' that thing off the ground," I said, shaking my head.

"Just you watch and learn."

I blinked and almost missed it. Still backing away, he released the kite gently as a gust of wind came from over Jim's shoulders and caught the kite head-on. Slowly, it began to rise.

"Pull on it, Jim, pull on it!" Gil called. "Keep up the tension!"

Young Jim's eyes were locked on the dragon kite as it rose in the sky, the long streamers from its flapping tail waving wildly in the wind. A broad smile covered the boy's face.

"Well done," I said, smiling myself.

"Feed it a little," Gil said, closing the distance

between where he stood and the boy quite quickly. "Give it a little more string and it'll rise. Good. Just like that. Look at it go!"

Without looking, Gil took the reel back from me and stepped up beside the boy, offering further advice as he saw fit. His lion kite was still higher, but Jim's dragon was rising rapidly. It took me a moment to realize it was rising perhaps a little *too* rapidly.

"Watch it, Gil, it looks unsteady there."

"He's right, Jim. Careful. You're in a rough patch. There's a building there, see? and when you're behind a building like that you get caught in turbulence. Careful now. The wind kicks off the top of that building and–watch out!"

The dragon caught a bad break and took a sharp turn for the ground, the pointed nose towards a beer-bellied gent with a ponytail who was packing up his beach bag.

I cupped my hands around my mouth and shouted, "Hey buddy, watch out there's a–"

In retrospect, I probably shouldn't have started with the "hey buddy" part, time sensitive as the warning was. Before I could even get the rest of it out, young Jim's dragon winged Ponytail across the shoulder before burying itself in the sand.

"Holy crap, man, are you all right?" Gil asked. It was just a kite after all–not exactly an anvil–but the wind had whipped it up fast enough to be able to do a bit of damage when it hit the guy.

"What the hell?" He turned angry eyes in our direction. "What's your beef buddy?" he shouted. "This your kite?" He looked down, his eyes following the string from the dragon kite not back to Gil, but back to Jim.

"I'm sorry," I said. "That was our fault–"

"The hell it was!" Ponytail continued. "Is this your jerk-off kid?"

"Hey, fella, why not calm down, eh?" Gil said, stepping in front of Jim. "No cause for that now, all right?"

"Speak for yourself, old man," Ponytail hollered, taking a step towards Gil. "Your idiot kid just–"

I stepped in front of Gil and put my hand on Ponytail's bare chest. "Step back, please," I said, my police training coming to full bore.

"Step back? You shittin' me, baldy? Who are you, the old guy's first born? Let me at your pops."

Rather than move, I held my ground and pushed back harder. "You need to calm down, all right. It was an accident. The kid certainly didn't mean to hit you with his kite, and I'm sorry that it did. If you will calm down I'd be happy to buy you a beer and make it up to you, all right, friend?" It was my best shot at diplomacy, but close as I stood to the guy, I could tell he'd had his share of beers already.

"Buy me a beer," Ponytail muttered shaking his head. "Buy me a beer? That kid just hit me in the head with his stupid friggin' kite."

"He didn't hit you in the head–" Gil began.

"Gil," I said, cutting him off.

"–so I don't want no stupid beer, I wanna knock the old timer's block off, all right?"

"That's enough," I said, turning to Gil. "Gil, let's

go. We're leaving. Jim, where are your parents–"

Before I could finish, Ponytail hit me. He was drunk and untrained, so the punch surprised me more than anything else. I stumbled forward and bumped into Gil. Somewhere down the beach, I heard a woman scream. As I straightened up and turned, I caught Ponytail's second punch right in the face.

The problem with someone like me is that not only do I have a wicked temper, but I also have been trained by both the police and the military. I know how to handle myself. Also, since joining the Zeros, I'd begun to work out again, so the flab that had begun to overtake me in my old security job was beginning to disappear. Normally, these are good things. But let me tell you, nothing good comes from losing your temper with a drunken goon.

And at that moment, any lingering shred of self-control I'd been fighting to maintain decided to step out. I rounded on Ponytail and showed him a thing or two from my basic hand-to-hand combat training.

And just like that, our picturesque vacation hit a bit of a speed bump.

CHAPTER 2 YOU'RE GONNA NEED SOMEBODY ON YOUR BOND

Getting into a fight on the beach is not exactly the excitement you came for, reader, I know. Sorry. But how about jail? Have you ever been to jail? I can say that until that humid June afternoon, I had never had the dubious honor of being *behind* the bars.

Even in a sunny, tourist friendly town like Rehoboth, jail is not nice. I sat beside Gil on a long wooden bench inside a "big" twelve by twelve foot holding cell pocked with enough graffiti and obscene scribblings that the walls were beginning to resemble Jackson Pollock art. We each wore **PROPERTY OF REHOBOTH POLICE** t-shirts given that we were both arrested while shirtless. Apparently the Rehoboth police station was a no shirt, no shoes, no service kind of place.

"Do you think we're gonna get out of here soon?" Gil asked me for about the thirtieth time.

"I dunno," I said. "Did you really have to leave your wallet in your backpack?"

"Did *you* really have to leave you wallet in your beach tote?"

"It's not a beach tote, it's a beach *bag*. A Philadelphia Eagle's beach bag."

"Do you think that makes it sound tougher? Can a beach bag be tough?"

I sighed. "Apparently not."

Without money, our pending misdemeanor assault was turning into a long stay in the clink. Nearly two hours in and we'd played Twenty Questions eight times (Gil's selections had been Evel Knievel, Bela Lugosi, Fozzy Bear, and Hulk Hogan; that should tell you enough). Ponytail, the guy I'd gotten into a tussle with, was in a smaller cell adjacent to ours. Given the fact that he'd popped a .09 when he was hauled in, he'd been given the pleasure of the drunk tank–it looked a whole lot like our cell, except it smelled much more of urine. He was currently sleeping off his ten or so Miller Lites (complete with his own complimentary jailhouse tee).

"Why hasn't Finch checked the cell phone yet?" Gil asked.

"Better question is 'why hasn't Finch noticed we've been missing for two hours?'"

"Yeah, that's a good one, too."

"I guess that Kierkegaard is pretty gripping stuff."

Gil shrugged and stared out the small slit of a window cut high into the wall. Outside, a fierce gold glow of Atlantic sunset was pouring through, making me miss the sound of the ocean. Ponytail's snoring was no substitute.

After my cork popped on the beach and I started in on Ponytail, Gil must've done something, because when the pair of deputies pulled Ponytail and I apart, Gil was somehow dragged away with us. I had a slight cut on the ridge of my left cheek and a shiner beginning to frame it. Ponytail found himself a little worse for wear; deep in his drunk tank siesta, I could still make out his split lip and the crimson-stained cotton balls plugging each nostril.

Gil took a deep breath, perhaps about to begin another verse of "Show Me the Way To Go Home" when a rattle of keys heralded someone at the door.

He stood and gripped the bars, his most plaintive frown on his face.

"Abercrombie and Dylan," a stumpy deputy called out, apparently unable to keep the three of us straight.

"Yes, yes, yup. Right here, bro!" Gil called out, waving.

"Someone's here to bail you out."

"Yippeee!"

"Gil, will you cool it 'til we're outta here?"

"Yeah, okay, sorry."

In the drunk tank, Ponytail sat bolt upright à la Frankenstein and shook his head. "Who?" he said. "What?"

"Cool off, Brady," the deputy said, walking towards our cell, keys in hand. "You've got a ways to go yet. Your wife said she'd bail you when you've sobered a bit."

Gil flipped Ponytail a double-bird with a "*WOOOO!!*" as our cell door was opened and we were escorted past him. He squinted at us, and I half expected him to drag a finger along his throat like a cartoon villain promising doom. He didn't. Instead, he laid back down and was snoring before we'd left the room.

In the cool, air-conditioned hallway of the police station, our deputy deposited us on a wooden bench slightly nicer than the one we'd just vacated. We were handcuff-free, but the **PROPERTY OF REHO-BOTH POLICE** tees were a bit more conspicuous than I preferred.

"Wait here a minute," our deputy said before disappearing into an office and shutting the door behind him.

"Weird that we're waiting," I said.

"Why?"

"No cuffs, no escort, no nothing. That doesn't make sense."

"We're in some Barney Fife station in the middle of nowhere–"

"No, man, you're wrong across the board here."

"Huh?"

"From what I've seen, this place is run okay. Sitting here makes me think that–"

"There you are," a cool voice interrupted me.

I looked up to see Finch, Gil's backpack over one shoulder and my beach bag over the other. "Ahh, yes," I said. "It makes sense now."

Finch nodded. "Did you really think I forgot about you?" he asked, apparently reading Gil's mind.

"Well, yeah," Gil said. "I mean, we been here for like... *hours and hours*, man."

"Just under two hours, I believe," Finch said.

"That how long it took to get ahold of Alfred?"

"Not Alfred," Finch said. "He was easy. But getting ahold of the right people down here was the challenge."

"What do you mean?" Gil asked, baffled.

"We're off the hook," I said.

"Huh?"

We'd worked a case involving Alfred Bascombe– a reasonably high-ranking politician in Philadelphia– and his wife Willa. We'd handled it with aplomb, and made friends in high places. Apparently just high enough.

"Alfred called somebody who called somebody who got us off," I said. "Right?"

"How'd he do that?" Gil asked. He held up his ink-stained hands. "I already got processed!"

"'Booked' is the word, Boss," I said. "But the right person can make anything go away." I felt more than a twinge of guilt admitting it. Having been a city cop, that kind of curried favor is a little disgusting to me, even when I'm the one profiting from it.

"That's rad," he said. "You think they'll let me have my mug shot? I'd frame that and hang it in my office."

"It may not send the right message to prospective clientele, Boss," Finch said.

Gil shrugged. "Then what are we still doing here?"

"I was told the sheriff wants to speak with us."

"Oh boy," I said, imagining some of the choice

words he'd have for us.

Gil opened his mouth but was interrupted by a muted shouting from beyond a door at the other end of the hallway. He frowned. "What's that, I wonder?"

The door opened and a second deputy came through, walking with purpose. He was taller than the first, with skin bronzed by the sun. He had his hat in hand and was sweating. Not sparing us even a glance, he opened a door on his left and stepped inside a rather small office, pulling the door shut behind him.

Well, almost shut. A two inch crack remained open, *just* enough to allow a collection of muted voices to escape.

"–don't care who they're friends with back in–"

"Sir?"

"–Philadelphia. Nobody is going to be starting–"

"Excuse me, sir?"

"–what is it?"

"There's been another one, Sheriff."

The office fell silent and I tried to imagine the face the local sheriff was making. Anger? Confu-sion? Shock?

"Where?" he said softly. *Shock.*

"Lewes. A young girl this time, sir. She–"

"How old?"

"Eleven."

A deep sigh. "Good lord."

"Loretta called just now and let me know. Apparently it happened early this morning. The girl's parents weren't sure if she'd run away or–"

"Same as the other," the Sheriff said, his voice still low. "My God what is happening? All right, I've gotta get on the horn to Mack and see if he needs anything."

"Sir?" the voice of our stumpy deputy chimed in.

"What is it Carter?"

"The prisoners are still outside. Would you like me to–"

"Goddamnit," the Sheriff grumbled. "I've got bigger... all right, bring 'em in, Carter. And you, Donnelly, you get me some info on this Lewes girl. We've gotta get Mack all the support we can muster, you hear? Help him when you finish with these fighters, Carter."

A pair of low affirmations followed before the office door opened and the two deputies strode out. Even the bronze one looked a little ashen.

Our deputy, henceforth known as Carter, beckoned us with his hand. "You three," he said. "Inside."

The three of us squeezed into the small office, Finch and Gil taking seats in the pair of guest chairs and me standing by the door.

When we stepped inside, the round, diminutive man behind the desk stood politely despite his obvious fluster. He had a sunburned face and thinning brown hair, and the dark circles under his eyes told me that the Sheriff found sleep to be an elusive mistress. A novelty name placard with a carved fisherman sat at his desk's edge, *SHERIFF R. LEE HUGGINS* carved into it.

"Pull that shut, will you, Gigantor?" Sheriff Huggins asked me as he resumed his seat.

I did, and waited. The office was small and clean, decorated with only one personal touch: on his blotter was one small framed picture of the Sheriff as a young man smiling beside a mustached younger man I imagined was his brother. Sheriff Huggins fussed with some papers on his desk before looking us over, his face hard but not cruel.

"I haven't... I haven't read the whole report Deputy Carter gave me on your altercation with Mr. Brady, but I'm not happy to have you here," he said. "In truth, I'm even less happy to have you leave under these circumstances."

None of us spoke. Gil probably felt bored, Finch couldn't have cared less, and I felt appropriate shame.

"I got a call from..." he checked a paper. "The Mayor's Chief of Staff. It's not a call I get everyday, especially in regards to a couple of guys involved in a physical altercation with an intoxicated man on the beach."

"He started it," Gil muttered.

Huggins gave Gil his best Dirty Harry gaze (and it wasn't half bad), under which Gil shriveled.

"Much as I hate to admit it, it does sound a bit like you put yourselves between this Brady character and a child; for that I thank you. But it doesn't pardon what you did."

He gave *me* the Dirty Harry look now. I deserved it.

"Men who understand the need to do what you

did should understand that there are better ways of resolving it than fighting." He lowered his eyes, apparently running out of energy in his parental scolding. He seemed exhausted and distracted, but trying like hell to give us half the attention he had previously decided we'd merited.

"I just..." he coughed, clearing his throat. "I don't want to see you in here again. This is a family town, and... I like it. I grew up here. Every year I do what I can to keep it the way I remember it, and every year it gets a little harder. Don't make it harder on me than it already is. All right?"

We all nodded, roughly in unison.

He shuffled some more papers. I expected an inspirational end to his guidance counselor schtick talking to, but it never came. He waved his hand dismissively. "Get outta here."

Gil and Finch stood, all too ready to evacuate.

"Sir?" I asked.

Huggins looked up at me. "What is it?"

"I know it's not my business, but I used to be a member of the force–"

"I could tell by the number you pulled on that Brady jackass," he interrupted.

"...uh, yes, sir. But my partners and I have worked with the police in Philadelphia before; we've helped them out on some tough cases, and–"

"We don't need any help from anybody," he said, preventing me from even finishing my sentence. "We can take care of our own, all right? I appreciate what you're trying to say, son... but I don't need your help."

I swallowed and nodded once. "Yes, sir. Understood."

He waved again. "That's it."

I wanted so much to object, to say something else. Before I could, Finch put his hand on my arm and said, "Let's go, Dylan."

I turned with my partners and left.

CHAPTER 3. ONLY THE BLUES

The door to the police station closed behind us with enough finality to leave me feeling just bad enough not to notice how crowded Rehoboth Avenue was.

"I could use an aqua velva, or one of those flaming volcano things," Gil said, his voice almost lost in the throng of pedestrians. "Or maybe a Zombie! Those are tasty!"

I looked up and saw a river of sunbaked tourists flowing past us, making their ways to hotel rooms, pizza joints, parked cars, or outdoor showers.

"Yeah."

The three of us fought our way against the crowd, moving from the west end of Rehoboth Avenue towards the ocean and boardwalk to the east. Rehoboth Beach is laid out pretty simply, a row of parallel streets leading up to the ocean with Rehoboth Avenue being the main hub of dining and shopping. The police station lay near the end of Rehoboth Avenue, giving us a long walk past t-shirt shops and old time photo stores before we got to the boardwalk.

My companions' silence in the police station surprised me, Gil in particular. The sheriff had been speaking with Deputy Carter about a missing child. Gil was usually unable to resist offering his assistance if he thought a kitten might be caught in a tree, and this was a lost kid. Was I missing something?

"You guys heard–"

"Not here," Finch said, cutting me off.

I took my bag back from Finch, pulling a pair of flip flops out in the process and slipped into them, choosing not to dwell on the fact that I'd been in a jail cell barefoot.

We passed the music pavilion at the head of Rehoboth Avenue and the ocean sprawled before us, a dark blue swatch lit by the sun slipping below the horizon at my back. The boardwalk opened up, following the beach to my left and right, filled with people. In the mix of voices and laughter, I could hear children screaming from the rides in the Funland pavilion further down the boardwalk. Despite the warmth of the June evening, I shivered.

"This way, pardners," Gil said, leading us about a block down the boardwalk to a bar on the second floor above a souvenir shop.

It was crowded, but we were lucky. We got a seat at the bar and ordered. Gil: piña colada, Finch: gin and tonic with lemon, me: Dogfish Head Namaste.

"Can we–"

"Hang on," Gil interrupted, turning to rifle through his bag.

I looked at Finch, but he sipped his G&T stonily, ignoring me. I didn't know what to do, so I followed his lead, taking a deep gulp of my beer. It was good, but not good enough to get the bad taste out of my mouth.

"Listen, are we gonna–"

Gil raised a finger and held a dialed phone to his ear. "Dot, hey it's me. Listen up, I need you to look into something for me." He looked around the bar, checking for prying eyes or ears, and lowered his voice. "Looks like they're having some children going missing down here. I need you to dig into this for me and get a big info dump together."

I cooled off, realizing what was happening. I turned halfway around on my stool and looked out at the ocean, now a dark navy, lost in shadow as it was. I listened to Gil and took another sip, realizing we were going to get into this. The Namaste tasted better already.

When he hung up, he turned to his piña colada and pulled the wedge of pineapple off the top, taking a wet bite from it. Juice ran down his chin and flecks of the fruit stuck in his bushy mustache.

"So we're gonna get involved, right?"

Gil chewed and smiled. "Do you know me at all?"

Beside me, even the stoic Finch cracked a smile– if only just. The thought crossed my mind that it was fortuitous, us getting arrested. There was another part of me that wondered if getting arrested wasn't something Gil did when he was bored to see if he could involve himself in some do-gooding, even in his downtime. Just a theory, but he's done weirder things. Not that it mattered at this point in either case.

"Dot's gonna get the info together for us; I told her to involve Willa if need be. You know how good your friend is with digging up stuff."

"She's not *my* friend," I said, a tad defensively. "She's *our* friend." Apparently my old crush had been not as secret as I'd believed. But alas, she was happily married.

Gil chuckled. "Yeah, okay. Anyway, she's gonna get it together, and when we get back to the hotel, I'll use their fax. They've got a fax, right?"

"I would imagine," Finch said.

"I like fax machines," Gil said. "I like the noises they make."

"I know, Boss," Finch said.

"So what kind of resources are there here, Dylan?" Gil asked me.

"What do you mean?"

"We're a little ways from our home base, so is there a library or something in the event we need to research stuff?"

"Sure, there's a library. It may be a little heavier on beach reading, but they've got one. Although, you know there's a chance this isn't supernatural, right?"

Gil scoffed. "Isn't supernatural? Hah! You're pretty funny, D. I forget sometimes that you're still the new guy."

Finch ignored Gil and looked at me. "It could be, what do the kids say... vanilla?"

"What?" I said. "'What the kids say'? What kids does he know?" I asked Gil.

"His *girlfriend*, remember?" he said, lowering his voice and snickering. "She's like... twenty something?"

"Oh, yeah, that would definitely explain it."

"–so, it could be non-supernatural," Finch continued, unbothered by our digression. "But the odds are against it."

"Why are the odds against it?"

"Because kidnapping one child is usually a crime perpetrated by a sexually deviant miscreant. Kidnapping multiple children means it has deeper, perhaps still darker roots."

"Why?"

"Because children are pure and have an unfettered joy and curiosity inside of them. There are those who believe themselves able to manipulate that and extract power from it."

I was a little taken aback by Finch speaking with such uncharacteristic whimsy. "Power?"

Finch nodded and sipped his gin and tonic. "That is correct. Whether or not the ability to siphon that joy actually exists is open to debate, but there are still a great many who believe it does and attempt it."

"So you're thinking definitely supernatural?"

"Definitely supernatural, big man," Gil said, clapping my shoulder. "So that's why I need to know what kind of resources they have down here."

"I need a little help in this regard," I admitted. "What do you mean? We've already met the cops," I looked down at my **PROPERTY OF REHOBOTH POLICE** shirt. "That didn't go as well as it could have."

"No, no, no, think *other*world, Dylan," Gil said.

"Who have we worked with?" Finch asked, prodding me in the right direction, perhaps the next step in my Zeros training. "Think about Dr. Ponderosa or Dr. Hanas. Think about the Guardians and the Death Collectors."

"Um, okay. Let me think."

"Excuse me, miss," Gil said, catching the eye of the young bartender; the name tag on her shirt read *Becky*. She smiled at him, either a reflex or the obvious reaction when you saw his beet-red face and farmer's tan.

"Another?" she asked, eyeing his mostly-full piña colada, complete with two umbrellas and a pineapple slice the size of my beer's coaster.

"Oh not yet, no. Lemme ask you, what is there fun to do around here?"

"You look like the Funland-type," she said, hitting the nail on the head.

"I do like bumper cars," Gil said. "Skee-ball too, that's for sure. But my friend here," he said, elbowing Finch, "is into crazy stuff. Like freaky stuff." He looked at Finch. "What did you say? Not vanilla."

Becky raised both hands and smiled awkwardly. "Whoa, um, I think I'm not... uh. There's probably someone here into that kinky stuff, but–"

"No," I said. "He's really not good at... well, speaking. Not kinky stuff. Wow, not at all, no."

"Kinky?" Gil asked, genuinely confused.

Finch stepped up, removing awkward from the equation. "Becky, where would I go if I wanted to get my fortune told, for example?" He put on his most charming smile and hit a home run. Apparently he'd learned a lot over the past few hundred years of his life about being charming when he needed to be.

"Oh," the bartender said, easing a little. "All right, I can help you with that. I thought you meant–"

"No," Finch said, smiling again. "No judgement, of course, but that's not what I meant."

The bartender nodded and began wiping down a glass. "There's not a lot around here, but more than meets the eye. And I'm not just talking about buying crystals or water pipes at Superkind."

"All right, Becky," Finch said, smiling once again. "What do you suggest?"

She smiled, putting the glass down. "I know just the place."

CHAPTER 4. WILD WITCH LADY

We ate some quick bar food and tipped Becky big before exiting into the night. I knew Rehoboth best, so I took Becky's vague directions and got us where we were going with minimal unexpected detours. A few twists and turns away from the bright lights and crowded buzz of Rehoboth Avenue took us into the tree-lined surrounding residential streets of our destination.

Madame Clarissa Explains It All, the sign read. It was purple neon and hung in a quaint bungalow's front window, a quaint bungalow that had seen some better days. Parts of the yard were overgrown in explosions of crab grass; the parts that weren't overgrown were only under control because all the plant life had died.

"Nice place," Gil said. He pointed at the sign. "Wasn't that a TV show?" he asked. "I think I got it on DVD."

"I am not familiar with a program about Madame Clarissa," Finch said.

There was a note hanging on the front door that looked like it had been made on a home computer. In bland Times New Roman it read, "Palmistry, fortune telling, tarot reading, astrological predictions, matchmaking, tea leaf readings, and divining of all kinds. Not for entertainment. Appointments preferred."

"What, no walk-ins?" I asked.

"If my barber takes walk-ins," Gil said, climbing a set of rickety steps, "Madame Clarissa takes walk-ins." He twisted the knob and stepped inside. Finch and I followed a few paces behind.

If I hadn't paid attention to the purple neon sign, I would have thought I was in an accountant's waiting room instead of a psychic's. Everything was white or gray, with even beige apparently being too exciting for Madame Clarissa. A few world-weary chairs surrounded a scratched IKEA coffee table covered with magazines like *Home & Garden* and *Cosmopolitan*. Even the "mysterious" curtains leading into Madame Clarissa's inner sanctum were grey. The place couldn't have been less offensive–or interesting–if it tried.

"Where's the creepy animal skull shrine?" Gil asked, smirking. "What about a sculpture of the Fates or some Yanni music?"

"Is it weird I used to listen to Yanni?" I asked distractedly as I shuffled a few magazines around on the table.

"You *what?*" Gil asked, his eyes wide.

"Yeah, you know an ex-girlfriend of mine–"

"The Boss's musical proclivities aside, Dylan, if I were you I would not be so quick to admit such a fact," Finch said with a ghost of a smile. "Even I know that."

"Do you even listen to music?" I asked him.

"Yes," Finch sighed. "Classical. Preferably early romantic."

"Of course you listen to classical music."

"Yeah," Gil said, "He likes classical. And don't forget AC/DC and Dragonforce and Iron Maiden and Týr and Blue Öyster Cult and Zep–"

"Have you ever said something and regretted it immediately?" I asked.

Gil frowned. "No," he said. "Not ever. But then again, I've never admitted liking Yanni."

"Can we get back to the point?" I suggested hopefully.

"Yes," Finch said. "Please."

On a small end table between a pair of chairs was a novelty lighthouse lamp and a few of Madame Clarissa's business cards. Completing the trifecta of weird was a bell, the kind you found on hotel lobby desks.

"Ah, brilliant!" Gil said as he slapped the bell gleefully with a loud *DING*.

"And what are we doing here exctly?" I asked, lowering my voice. "Did anyone ever explain that to me?"

Gil smiled. "Saving lives, my man," he said. "You'll... well, just wait and see."

"Saving lives, all right. So we're not looking for tonight's Powerball?"

With a dramatic flourish, the grey curtain in the corner was swept aside, revealing a wild-haired middle-aged woman who had–how shall I put this... crazy eyes? Curly ginger hair exploded from her head like it was trying to escape, and to complete the crazy she wore a brightly colored floral muumuu.

"I do not provide Powerball numbers," she said, her voice warbling loudly in an insane sing-song way. "Did you not see the sign in my front window?"

"The one about appointments?" Gil asked.

"Not the one about appointments! The sign about this not being entertainment! Although the sign about appointments seems relevant now, as well!"

"True," Gil said. "But we were in the neigh–borhood, so–hey I like your shirt!"

"Oh, well, thank you." She looked down at her muumuu and seemed to soften a bit. "It's not a shirt, but–what can I do for you, gentlemen? Have you... come for spiritual guidance?"

"No, not really," I said, thinking about the missing child and wanting nothing more than to get back to the hotel and get Dottie's incoming fax. "We're here for–"

"As a matter of fact," Gil said, "that's *exactly* why we're here. Some good ol' spiritual guidance."

"Oh?" she asked, eyeing me. "Your friend seems a little... resistant."

"Forgive him," Finch smiled. "Our associate is slow to accept the... well, *mystic arts*." He chose his words carefully. I looked at Gil and raised an eye-brow. He winked dramatically.

"No need to apologize," our host said. "He will come to understand the depths of the arts soon enough." She bowed. "I am Madame Clarissa!" she said. "Welcome!"

"It is our pleasure, Madame," Finch said, bowing slightly. "My name is Alistair Finch and this is my boss Giles Abercrombie."

"Very happy to meet you, ma'am," Gil said, tipping the brim of an invisible hat. "This here is our associate, Dylan."

"Hi," I said. "Charmed."

Madame Clarissa looked me over, a sour and suspicious look on her face. "Likewise," she said. She turned to Gil and Finch and smiled. "You gentlemen are quite welcome. I apologize for the rather frosty introduction, I... well, don't get many *believers* here. Mostly I find myself pursuing the arcane knowledge alone... and getting mocked by tourists–and locals." She admitted the last part quietly, almost under her breath, but I heard her nonetheless and immediately felt bad. It was easy to laugh at her, but there was something undeniably genuine about her, as well.

"We're not here to mock," Gil said. "Just for a little help and guidance."

"Of course, my children of Hecate. Guidance is my purpose. I am happy to provide whatever assistance I am able. Which of you gentlemen would like to go first?"

"As a matter of fact..." Finch began, the ghost of a smile tugging at the corner of his mouth.

"...it's our doubting buddy here," Gil finished, a broad smirk covering his face as he pushed me forward. "He wants you to read his palm or somethin'."

"Your... eh... friend?" Madame Clarissa said frowning. "Why... I'm happy to, but... well, why do you want me to sit down with a skeptical mind, brothers?"

"Only one way to become a believer!" Gil said.

"I believe my friend is correct in this supposition," Finch agreed. "Wouldn't you say, Madame Clarissa?"

"I don't know," I said. "I think Miss Clarissa, er, *Madame* Clar–"

"No," Madame Clarissa interrupted. "I think you are exactly right!" She turned to me, a determined look on her face. "Mr. Dylan? Please, step into my mystic realm!"

"Mystic? Uh..." I looked back at Gil and Finch as the psychic took my hand and lead me towards her inner sanctum. I caught Gil's eye and shook my head. He smiled and nodded encouragingly.

"Now is the time to come to the light, big guy," he said, grinning.

"Yes, indeed," Finch added, a real shit-eating smile gracing his face. "No time like the present, is there?"

Before I could manage some whip-smart retort, I was led through the grey curtain and found myself in the "mystic realm," which to Madame Clarissa meant a small office lit by lava lamps (seriously) and furnished with bean bag chairs and a card table covered by an *Alice in Wonderland* tablecloth. A star chart was thumb-tacked to the ceiling and hung limply. Behind the bean bag on which she plopped, a beaded curtain covered a window overlooking a small overgrown backyard.

"Listen," I said. "I don't think this–"

"Sit, Mr. Dylan, please," she said, indicating the facing bean bag. "This won't hurt a bit!" she said with a generous smile. A splash of lipstick was slashed across her front teeth. She may have been the first person to employ the use of the exclamation point more generously than Gil.

"All right," I said with a sigh, lowering myself to the bean bag and resting my hands on the table.

From a table in the corner, she poured a small cup of hot tea and took a sip, all the while watching me.

When she was finished she said, "Let me see your hands." She reached across towards me. I turned my hands palm up and extended them to her.

"Your life line is quite well-defined!" she said, nodding. "And it intersects with the headline, as it should. Are you involved with someone?" she asked, her eyes sly.

"No," I said, maybe a little too quickly.

She smiled. "Perhaps you'd only *like* to be involved with someone," she said, returning her attention to my hand before I could respond, "because you've quite a strong union line, as well!"

"Well, I don't know anything about that, but..."

"This is strange," she said, pulling my left hand closer. "Your fate line is rather unique. Here, you see this?" she said, pointing.

"No..."

"This line here," she said, pulling my hand closer. "This is your fate line. It runs up the center of your palm. It's strange. It's quite busy. You see, it has breaks in it... breaks and islands. Unfortunately, young man, that means that your life will not always be easy. I'm terribly sorry to inform you of this."

"Oh jeez. That can't be good!" I said, trying to be a good sport. So far, she'd said nothing specific in the least, only tossing out a bunch of generic statements that could be applied to pretty much anyone. Yeah, I'd seen things while working as a Zero to make me a "believer," but I'd not seen enough to be converted to palmistry–not yet, at least.

She took another sip of tea. "And these lines," she continued, licking her lips. "They intersect perpendicularly with your line of fate. That means that you will be opposed at some point. Opposed by another."

"Yeah, like the tax man or a crazy ex-girlfriend or–"

"No," she said, her voice lowering ominously. "More than that! Someone determined to stop your life's progress."

"Huh," I said. In a different line of work, that might mean a guy at the office was after my promotion. In my line of work, that usually meant someone wanted to bury me. "Unfortunately, I think you could be right about that," I said.

"That's enough of that!" she said, releasing my hand. "I believe I'm coming to understand you, Mr. Dylan. I'm beginning to feel your aura!"

"Oh, that's good," I said, wishing Gil and Finch were in here so I could strangle them. "Feeling auras is good."

She nodded and finished her cup of tea. With a

wildly dramatic flourish that was coming to define Madame Clarissa, she gave the empty glass a strong shake.

"What are you–"

"Tasseography, Mr. Dylan! Reading the tea leaves!" When she was finished shaking the cup, she turned it upside down over her saucer, releasing a final dribble of tea. She turned the cup over and stared down into it.

I rested my chin on my hand. "Okay, what do you see?"

"I see... I see..."

"Hmm?"

"A chessman!"

"Oh good!"

"That's not a good thing, young man. A chessman means there are difficulties coming!"

"Ah, of course."

"And here, here is the shape of a bear."

"A teddy bear?"

"No, a–" she stopped and spared a moment to glare at me. "A bear means that a difficult person is in your future. You should know much about that, Mr. Dylan."

I smiled.

"And here, here is a fan. Fan's show coquetry! And social dalliances."

"Coquet-what?" I asked, picking something out of my teeth with my fingernail.

"Did you hear the second thing? Social

dalliances? It's like flirtation."

"Ah, okay."

"And this," she said, continuing around the glass clockwise, "this is a wheel."

"Oh no, not a wheel."

"There will be things beyond your control that will change your life. Ah, but I believe a reliable friend will see you through."

"That's good." I started to lean back before I remembered the beanbag did not have a backrest. I almost went backwards, ass over teacups, before I stopped myself.

"But this here, this X is a sign of defeat and loss! I... I can't tell if you will overcome..."

"Probably," I said, shrugging.

"It is beside an empty basket. An empty basket near the handle of the cup..."

"Hmm?"

"A dear friend of mine believes that means a missing child," she said softly.

"What?"

She looked down at the cup. "This mask means you are being deceived–"

"Wait, what about a child?"

"All I see is what the leaves show me! Here is the overcome defeat, here is the lost child, and here, here is a troublesome secret... and finally..."

"I wish you could tell me more about the empty basket."

"...here is a hated enemy beside a squirrel."

"*What?*"

"The squirrel means success after hardships!"

"Of course it does," I groaned.

"Illuminating!"

"Yeah, illuminating, all right. Baskets, squirrels, chessmen, wheels, fans... there's a lot of shit in that cup."

She set the cup down, ignoring me. I tipped it towards me, revealing streaks and splashes of what looked like dirt. Not much else. Definitely no squirrels.

I sighed.

"Now!" she said. "Time for the reading of the tarot!"

"That's nice," I said, checking my watch. The one thing I'd been interested in hearing was nothing but a passing remark.

She pulled a small box from beneath the table and from it removed cards, yellow with age. Carefully, her plump hands began to shuffle.

All right, I admit it, my mind wandered. I thought about the missing kids and what our next step would be. I thought about that pony-tailed guy on the beach I'd decked earlier and I thought about Willa. Hell, I even thought about who was next up in the Phillies pitching rotation. I thought about pretty much everything other than Madame Muumuu.

"This is not good," she said, interrupting my reverie and bringing me back down to Earth.

"Huh? Wha?" I said, blinking a few times and looking down at the table.

A few cards were turned over, but her attention was locked on one card in particular, one with a rather striking image, at that.

"The Tower," she said, her voice low and stricken. "I must say, Mr. Dylan, that is not good, I'm afraid."

"What is it?"

"The Tower represents a shocking change. It is epitomized by chaos. It means that something terrible will happen, but with it will come a certain measure of enlightenment. With destruction comes creation, never forget that."

"'A shocking change epitomized by chaos,' huh? That is fantastic." I wasn't buying the tarot stuff, but did I really need to pick the crappiest Death card on my first time out?

"As a matter of fact," Madame Clarissa said, "the Death card is really not that bad. It's more to do with change than anything else."

"Oh?" I asked, interested for the first time. It took me a minute to realize I hadn't spoken that thought out loud. "Wait a second..." I said. "Did I... say that out loud? No, I didn't..."

She looked up and blushed. "Apologies, Mr. Dylan," she said. "I... well, sometimes I *hear* more than I mean to."

"Um, yeah, okay," I said, genuinely freaked out. "I, uh..." I checked my watch again, at this point ready to get the hell out of there. I still wasn't sure what Gil and Finch had hoped I would learn with Madame Weirdo, but at this point I was ready to leave. "Is there anything else?"

She looked at me, turning her head slightly askance, as if she was measuring me up. *Did you really read my mind?* I thought as loudly as I could. Odds are that she just guessed. It only took one perfect coincidence to turn a non-believer into a believer, right? Had she staked it all on that and won? Or was she listening to my doubting thoughts even then?

"Give me your hand once more," she said abruptly, a seriousness washing away the dramatic facade.

"I thought you already read my palm?" I asked.

"I don't want to read your palm," she said. "This is not for me, Dylan. This is for you."

My hands stayed in my lap.

"Please," she said.

I reached across the table once more.

When we touched, it was like an electrocution. And this time, I was reading *her* mind.

CHAPTER 5. SAND AND FOAM

All right, I bugged the hell out of there. Maybe a calmer guy would be able to just get up and make an exit.

I could not.

I ripped through the grey curtain, rushing back into the waiting room. Gil and Finch were seated in the corner. Finch sat calmly with his eyes closed. Gil paged wide-eyed through an issue of *Cosmopolitan.*

"Let's go," I said. "Now. Right now."

They shot bolt upright.

"What happened?" Gil asked. "You all right? You look like you just chopped jalapeños and touched your—"

"Boss," Finch interrupted. "That's not a good thing to say. What did we talk about?"

"Oh, what? I just—"

"Let's go," I said. "Now. Now. Right now." I barely finished the sentence before I pushed open the door and stepped outside. Over my shoulder I saw Finch pull his wallet from his pocket and leave a few bills on the table beside the lighthouse lamp and business cards.

Outside, crickets were chirping fiercely in the darkness. Half a block away, a group of kids were stumbling down the street, laughing. I wiped a hand across my forehead and felt nothing but sweat. Cold sweat.

Behind me, Madame Clarissa's door banged shut as Gil and Finch tumbled out after me.

"What is it? What happened, big man?" Gil asked.

"Let's move. I have to get away from here right now. I am... I'm a little overwhelmed and more than a little freaked out."

"Okay, yeah sure, that's–"

I didn't wait to hear the end of that. I moved quickly ahead, passing houses as lights began turning off. I'm not sure how long we were in there, but long enough. The streets were thinning as people returned to their rentals and condos, dragging with them their crying kids and prizes from the game pavilion.

At the end of the street we emerged on the north end of the boardwalk, not far from the Henlopen Hotel that bookended the very northern edge of the boardwalk. I took a seat on a bench that overlooked the ocean and tried to catch my breath.

Gil sat on my right, Finch on my left.

For a few minutes, no one said anything, a beautiful product of working with these guys long enough for them to get to know me a little. I'd be fine, I just needed a minute.

I cleared my head and watched the ocean, shrouded mostly in darkness, move slowly up the beach, leaving a trail of bubbling white water and foam on the sand as it receded.

I took a deep breath and frowned. I looked at Gil. Sitting contentedly on the bench, he had lit his pipe. A foul smelling cloud of pipe smoke billowed around us.

I waved my hand. "Where do you get that stuff?" I asked. "It's awful."

"Hey, I don't complain about your jazz music when you put it on. People should never be made to feel bad about things that make them happy."

He puffed a few more times, and I watched the ocean. Behind us, the footfalls of passersby became more and more sporadic.

"You guys knew something would happen, right?" I asked.

Gil looked at me but didn't speak, he only chewed his pipe.

"We did not know," Finch said, "but we suspected."

"What was it?"

"We figured the vael would do something," Gil said. "We figured that if the lady was legit and she was probing you, the vael would... well, probe back."

"It did," I said.

"I requested that we not tell you, Dylan," Finch said. "Your mastery of the vael has been... uneven. I feared that if you went in knowing what we wanted to happen, then–"

"I'd choke, right?"

My friends didn't say anything, maybe the most damning response of all. The problem was that they were right. I just couldn't seem to get the hang of the powers I'd only just learned were inside me. I'd been feeling like the Hulk of late. Only when I lost control could I begin to manipulate the vael. Tapping into its power was so inconsistent when I tried otherwise.

"Can't say I blame you," I said. "Just be straight with me, all right?"

"Told you it was a bad idea," Gil grumbled. "But *noooooo*, no one ever listens to me! I'm just the boss or whatever."

On my left, Finch shrugged. "We got what we needed."

I sighed, always surprised at Finch's cold pragmatism. "Anyway," I said. "Do you want to know what I learned?"

"Of course!" Gil said.

"Okay, well it turns out that Madame Clarissa is a bit of an... ostracized Wiccan?"

"A witch!" Gil exclaimed.

"I'm not honestly sure if 'witch' is considered PC in their circles, or what..." I said. "But essentially, yes. And Rehoboth has a small but dedicated collec-tion of witches, it would seem."

"Are there covens?" Finch asked. "You said she'd been ostracized."

"There is one coven," I said, "and Clarissa was ostracized from it because of how she makes her living."

"Okay, let's focus on that," Gil said. Smiling, he put on a terrible Glenda the Good Witch voice. "Are they good witches?" he squeaked. "Or bad witches?"

"She didn't say... or think? Or did she? Did I read her mind?"

"Sort of," Gil said. "Sort of I think? I'm not really sure, honestly."

"I believe the vael did read her mind, yes," Finch said. "That was exactly what we hoped, remember? If she was a legitimate Wiccan then she would be trying to enter your mind. The vael's sense of self-preservation would take steps to learn more and protect itself as necessary."

"All right," I said, shaking my head. "So what did you want to know?"

"The coven," Gil said. "What's the deal with the coven?"

"Well, I don't know where they are, and neither does Clarissa, but she..."

"She what?" Finch asked.

"She is afraid of them. And she knows about the missing kids."

"How?"

I closed my eyes and listened to the sea; it made this easier. "The first was widely reported in local papers. The second..." I racked my mind, trying to remember everything I'd learned in one loud *BURST* of information. "She has a police scanner. Upstairs in her house. She listens to it when she's not working."

"What do the kids have to do with–"

"She is afraid the coven has something to do with the disappearances."

"Why?" Finch pressed.

I bit my lip. The images were beginning to cloud over and lose their focus, as if they were sinking in dark water. "There was evidence left at the first scene."

"What kind of evidence? Who found it? When?"

Finch was asking the questions faster and faster, realizing that I was losing it.

"Some kind of talisman... the deputy found it the next morning. And an eye witness–"

"Who?"

"A concierge. A night concierge at a hotel in Lewes where the child was taken."

"What did he see?"

"A figure... a tall, thin woman dressed in black robes."

"What has Clarissa done?"

"What?"

"If she suspects, she will act," Finch said. "She owns a scanner and has done research on the coven. What has she done to involve herself?"

"She investigated the first scene the night after the first kidnapping."

"And the second? What about the second?"

My brain felt like a grape that had yielded all the juice it could. Still, I pressed. "I think..."

"Yes?"

"She is... yes. She is planning on going out tonight to search the area."

"Where, Dylan?"

"Fort Miles in the Henlopen State Park."

"When? When will she be there?"

I caught the last piece of information, just before it was carried away on the tide. "She plans to leave at 3AM." I released a deep breath I had apparently been holding.

"Perfect," Finch said. "Thank you."

"Boy, that was *bracing*," I said.

"When Finch is on the scent, he's mighty persistent," Gil said with a smile. He took a satisfied puff of his pipe.

I nodded, still watching the ocean. The experience with Madame Clarissa had left me a little buzzed, and I could feel my heart banging in my chest like a timpani.

"You all right?" Gil asked.

"Yeah," I said. "I just realized."

"What?"

"I was wrong about Clarissa. I thought she was a joke. Just like everybody else does. But she's not. She's been trying to find the missing kid. And now another has been taken."

"You made a mistake," Finch said. "But you won't make it again."

"It's not that," I said. Of course Finch would look on guilt as misplaced disappointment in under-estimating an adversary. "I treated her the same as the townies and vacationers do: badly. It never occurred to me that she was legit. It didn't occur to me that she was doing good, or at least trying."

"Well, you can apologize when you see her," Gil said.

"What do you mean?"

"Of course, we're going to the park tonight," he said. "Duh. We're gonna go looking for evidence of evil witches, my man! And with a good witch, too!!"

CHAPTER 6. GET THY BEARINGS

"I think we can go back north on this Route 1 thing, past those outlets, and make a right somewhere? Does that sound right?" Gil asked.

"I told you, I know how to get there," I said.

"Yeah, but I don't wanna get lost. We can't be late, man."

"I'm not gonna get lost," I assured him.

Gil was laying on his stomach across the king size bed, a pair of reading glasses on the end of his nose, a map of Delaware spread out in front of him. Beside the map was a stack of Oreos, liberated from their packaging. His feet were up behind him, crossed at the ankle, a pose that was extremely reminiscent of a teenaged girl.

"You can see why I'd worry, though, right?" He looked up at me, frowning. "These roads are all so *small*."

"They're gonna be a little bigger while we're driving," I said. "Maps don't do roads much justice."

"Hmph," Gil muttered.

"Are you gonna take a nap or something?" I asked. "It's almost midnight and if–"

"I'm waiting for Finch to bring Dottie and Willa's

intel when it comes through. But apparently this joint's fax is a little slow."

"Why not wait in your room?" I suggested. "I could really go for a nap before we're out all night."

"Nah, I'm cool here." He took off his reading glasses and grabbed the TV remote, flipping through channels listlessly. "Thanks, though," he said, popping an Oreo into his mouth.

I looked longingly at my bed, wishing I was sleeping in it instead of dozing in the room's lumpy desk chair.

"Oooh," Gil said, dropping his remote. "Wrestling!"

"You watch wrestling–?"

The door swung open, interrupting my muttering, and Finch strode into the room, a pile of paperwork in hand.

"Finally," I said. "What took you so long?"

"Don't get me started on the telecommunication capabilities of a resort town. I do believe I could have acquired this information faster by driving to Philadelphia and picking it up in person."

"If you could drive," Gil said, eating another Oreo.

"If I could drive," Finch conceded.

"Or maybe someone should have brought the laptop," I said.

"A lap-who?" Gil asked.

"I was told this was vacation," Finch scowled. "I wasn't expecting–"

"*Anyway*," I interrupted. "What did Dottie find?"

Finch peeled a bundle of papers off the top and handed them to me. "Unfortunately, not much. Dottie's research has borne little more than what you may find in an *Encyclopedia Britannica*. Population, climate, population density."

"*Wikipedia*. Say *Wikipedia*, Finch," I said. "You're showing your age."

"Whatever. Her research has essentially produced the same information the internet utility Google would. Research not being Dottie's specialty."

"Her heart is willing," Gil said, "but yada yada yada..."

"Did you really just say 'internet utility'?" I asked, shaking my head.

"What about Willa?" Gil asked, muting the TV.

"Mrs. Bascombe found more, but still, not much." He handed Gil the remaining papers. "Although she had some choice words to say about using a fax machine." He glared at Gil. "Email would have been so much simpler."

I watched Gil peruse the papers Finch had handed him. "Why does he get the good stuff?"

"Because I'm the boss, big man," he said with a grin. He dropped a cookie and returned his reading glasses to his nose, frowning. "This is it?"

"It gets worse, actually," Finch said, pointing.

"What?" I asked.

Gil groaned and handed me the paper. It was a shoddy photocopy of a news story.

"An article?" I said, taking the paper from him. It was the write-up on the first kidnapping. "That's better than nothing, though."

"Yeah, but look at this, though," Gil said, tapping the paper with a fingertip.

Just beyond his sun-burned finger were the words *"Continued on page A8."*

"Okay," I said. "What's the problem?"

Gil lifted a pair of empty hands.

"Where's the rest of it?" I asked.

"That's the problem, big guy!" Gil said.

"I called Willa," Finch said. "Unfortunately, it seems the paper does not keep very good digital records. In this case, only the first half of the article is available."

"Where's the rest?"

"I imagine it exists in hard copy," Finch said. "And if a digital file exists, it will probably be in the newspaper's office."

"What about the police files?"

"Again, now you understand why I am lamenting the current state of a beachside resort community's digital records."

"It's only on paper?"

"That's what Mrs. Bascombe explained to me."

"You gotta admit, big guy, they probably don't get a lot of high profile crime here. Do they really need to immortalize drunk and disorderly misdemeanors in the cloud?" Gil said.

"Do you even know what the cloud is?" I asked.

"Umm, no?"

I skimmed the article fragment in my hand. "It's a

puff piece," I said angrily. "This focuses on the location and unnamed eyewitnesses who last saw the child. Other than the child, no names are given. If there are any actual details, they're not here."

"Yes," Finch said. "Again, need I explain my disappointment in the current–"

"No," I interrupted. "I think we got it."

"What's next?" Gil asked. "Wanna take another shot at the Sheriff?"

"I'm pretty sure Sheriff Huggins would rather book us for assault and battery than hire us on as summer deputies," I said.

"Ah, yes, but that's where Mrs. Bascombe did not leave us empty-handed," Finch said.

"What do you mean?"

Smiling uncharacteristically, he proffered the last paper he held. I read it over. "What is this?" I said. "Is this really what it looks like?"

Finch nodded. "It is some information Mrs. Bascombe located on the Sheriff's deputy."

"What was his name..." Gil said, putting on his thinking-face and snapping his fingers. "Deputy... Carter? Is that right?"

"That was the other guy," I said. "This is someone named John Donnelly."

Finch nodded again. "John Donnelly is the newest deputy, hired five months ago. It turns out 'John Michael Donnelly' is a false name. A detailed background check run by the right people turned over just the right rocks, exposing all of this fellow's secrets."

"That's impossible," I said. "They run background checks when they hire these guys."

"You really think Willa's checks are the same as the standard background checks, big man?" Gil asked.

I shrugged. "Fair enough."

Finch continued. "Mr. John Michael Donnelly, aka William Lester Leachman, is wanted for questioning in the murder of his wife Eileen in Grundy County, Iowa in June 2003. Shortly after the crime, he disappeared."

"Whoa, hold on. How did this guy get a bogus identity that was solid enough to get past a state background check?" I asked, genuinely dumbfounded. "No way he bought that from some goon in Cedar Rapids."

"Frankly, I've no bloody idea," Finch said. "But Mrs. Bascombe is looking into it."

"What's the point of this dirty info?" Gil asked, looking over the paper. "Get that dude fired and try and get Sheriff Huggybear to hire the big man in his place?"

"I believe Mrs. Bascombe hoped the information could be used to ingratiate us to the Sheriff, perhaps putting us in his good graces."

"Fat chance," I said. "It's more likely to piss him off royally."

"We'll have to take our chances," Gil said. "It's the only leverage we've got."

"There's one more thing," Finch said.

"What's that?"

"When I spoke with Mrs. Bascombe, she had just acquired information regarding the most recent victim."

Neither Gil nor I spoke. The moment hung heavy. With Wrestlemania muted on the TV, Oreos in hand, sun-burns fresh on the skin, and the smell of suntan lotion rich in the air, it was terribly easy to forget that two children were missing, perhaps even dead. Vacation has a way of whisking away a per-son's perspective, and thankfully we'd just been reminded that despite the boardwalk music and the smell of taffy in the air, we were on the clock.

From his pocket, Finch removed a small piece of scrap paper, marked by his neat penmanship.

"Young miss Megan Wilson was reported missing at approximately 11:20 this morning. She is eleven years old and from Mount Airy, Pennsylvania. She is an A student at the Charles C. Henry school in Philadelphia and enjoys playing soccer."

Gil looked down at the scan of the news article. "This boy is ten. He is from Newark, Delaware. His name is Benjamin Mason, Jr." His eyes moved across the article. "His parents call him Benji."

Somewhere outside, a flash of heat lightning cast an ominous light over the beach town as the clock struck midnight.

Gil turned off the TV and sat up. "Get some rest," he said, "both of you. We'll leave here at 2. We've got work to do."

CHAPTER 7. THREE KINGFISHERS

All right, so we got lost.

Shut up.

Despite Gil's worries, it didn't happen on the drive. The trouble came when we parked, snuck into the park through a swampy glade full of mosquitos and cattails, and tried to locate the remains of Fort Miles in the dark. Unlike what you may have learned at the movies, stars and the moon together don't cast *quite* enough light to navigate a state park at 3AM. So yeah, we got lost.

At first, it was all right. We knew where we were (sort of), and we had a pretty good idea of where we were going. But as the minutes ticked past, we started getting edgy. We wanted to meet Clarissa while she was searching. Perhaps we could help her; perhaps we could form some kind of bond. After forty minutes of stumbling in the dark, I was beginning to figure neither of these things was even a possibility. The trouble was that we just couldn't seem to find the actual historic site. You'd think that it would be pretty easy to find a thirty-six foot gun with a twelve-inch barrel jutting from a concrete bunker carved into the side of a hill. It wasn't–at least not for us.

"What's that?" Gil asked, breathlessly.

"What's what?"

"I'm pointing," he huffed.

"I can't see a damned thing," I said, slapping at a mosquito on my neck.

"But I'm pointing!"

"It's dark."

"It's an observation tower," Finch said.

"You can see that?"

"Yes," he said simply.

"I can't see it, but if it's an observation tower," I said, "it was built during World War II to spot enemy u-boats and ships."

"Delaware was a pretty big target during WW2, eh?" Gil chuckled.

"Hey man, it's small but it did its part."

"Quiet," Finch interrupted.

"What?" Gil asked.

Finch didn't respond, but I could imagine the wicked stinkeye he was giving Gil in the dark.

In the darkness, I'd hoped my other senses would pick up some slack, but maybe it was the strong smell of salt in the air from the ocean or the soporific cadence of the waves; either way I was having a hard time focusing. The fact that it was almost 4AM didn't help.

"What is it?" I finally whispered.

"I could have sworn–" Finch began.

"Hey, hey!" Gil laughed. "Found me a concrete path over here, boys!"

"*Shhhh!*" I called, trying to quiet Gil as I stumbled towards his voice. "She doesn't know we're coming," I whispered. "We don't want to scare her away, remember?"

"Oh, yeah. There's that. Sorry."

"You've found a path?"

"Yeah!"

My foot slapped down against pavement, finally leaving the thick rustle of overgrown grass. "Thank the gods for that," I muttered, slapping bugs off my legs. "I'll be killing ticks for days. I'll be lucky if I don't get Lyme disease."

"Weren't you vaccinated?" Finch scolded. "Lyme disease vaccinations–"

A voice called from the darkness, interrupting Finch's healthcare lecture. "Ah, if it isn't the three kingfishers!"

"King what?" Gil asked. "Isn't that a fish?"

"The kingfisher is a bird," Finch said.

"Yes," the voice said, "the kingfisher is a bird. In some cultures it is a good omen, in others it is a bad omen. I've yet to decide if you three are good or bad."

I took a step towards the sound of the voice. "Clarissa?" I asked.

A flashlight came to life, shining down on us from above. "Yes," the voice said. "It has certainly taken you three long enough to arrive. I've been waiting."

***

With assistance from the flashlight, we climbed the knoll up onto the slight plateau upon which Fort Miles sat, finding Madame Clarissa seated on a low sandbag wall surrounding a long-barreled 8-inch gun. The gun was mounted directly into a concrete dais rather than an old-fashioned two-wheel chassis like it would have been during the war. Gone was her tropical muumuu. In its place was a skirt and tropical shirt with a jean jacket.

"That's some artillery!" Gil said, patting the barrel. "And that's another sweet shirt!"

"Did you know they only fired these guns once?" Clarissa said.

"Bummer," Gil said. "Speaking of bummer, how did you know we were coming?"

"Two things," Clarissa said. "One, you were making a remarkable amount of noise. I could hear you three walking all around the Fort for the past hour. If you hadn't found me when you did, I was about to start shouting."

"And the second thing?" I asked.

In the dim light cast by her flashlight, she smiled. "I'm a psychic," she said.

"Perhaps we should talk about that," Finch said.

Clarissa sighed. "All right, not really a psychic," she said. "I do have some mastery of supernatural forces, but I've no real powers of divination."

"You'll come to learn that the true word is 'otherworld,'" Finch said.

"Otherworld?" Clarissa asked, her voice low. "Then you understand this a bit more than I do. I understand very little," she said, "and I'm waiting for you because I knew you would come. Something happened when I gave your reading, Dylan. Can you... can you explain what happened–"

"When we touched?" I said. "I think we can, but that may be best saved for another time and place."

"I agree," Finch said. "Now that we are here and we have finally found you, I believe we should do what we came to do and leave. I fear the insects will soon carry us away."

I slapped at my neck again, a half-second too late. "I think that's actually a real threat."

"Why are you here?" Clarissa asked.

"Uh, you said you knew we were comin', right?" Gil asked.

"I... yes, I did. Like I said, something happened," Clarissa said. "When we touched, something was... I don't know, transferred? I was planning on coming here to look for clues, and when we touched, I knew you would come, too. I just knew it."

"We're here for the same reason you are," I said.

"Megan Wilson and Benjamin Mason," Gil said. "The kids."

"The *missing* kids," Clarissa said. "Then you know."

"Yeah."

"Why isn't this getting more press?" I asked. "Isn't it a bit strange for two children to go missing in a resort community?"

"It is strange," Clarissa said. "And I have no idea why it's not been more publicized. After Benji was taken, I waited for the news vans. I waited for the story to break. It never did. There was no coverage, no scandal, no nothing. When I heard about Megan being taken this morning, I didn't think it could be ignored again. I was wrong."

"Perhaps it's going to get picked up by–" I began.

"I called the Philadelphia stations and the Baltimore stations," Clarissa said. "Both blew me off. No one wants this story. And the police here can't get any help, not even from the state; it's like no one wants to acknowledge these crimes."

"Weird," Gil said, scratching his bushy mustache.

"It is," Clarissa said. "And I couldn't just do nothing, I couldn't. So I thought I'd come looking for clues. Sheriff Huggins is a good man, but he doesn't know what he's dealing with. He doesn't believe. He doesn't even know what to look for."

"What exactly *is* he dealing with?" I asked.

Clarissa sighed. "What do you know about witches?" she asked.

"Is 'witch' a PC term?" Gil asked. "We were wonderin' that earlier."

Clarissa's head hung low. "I don't know, honestly," she said. "When I first began to learn about the Earth Arts, I tried to join a coven of like women, but they would not have me because they found my profession... offensive. Their leader said I was exploiting their beliefs. They didn't understand that I only want to do good, I only want to help people."

Finch, apparently bored by Clarissa, began to wander, carefully taking in the historic site and exploring the craggy rocks that surrounded the battery of buildings.

"Do you think these witches have something to do with what's happening?" I asked.

"Don't you know about the reports?"

"What reports?"

"Eyewitness reports from each kidnapping. There are two reports from two different eyewit-nesses."

"I couldn't find any information at all on eye-witnesses," I said. "Our information was... lacking."

"A hotel worker told the police that he saw a tall, thin woman dressed in black with a long, pointy nose. And she had on a wide-brimmed hat."

I nodded as she spoke, remembering what I'd learned from our little mind-melding experiment.

"Pointy, right? Did she try to sell anyone a poisonous apple while she was at it?" Gil asked.

"I know it sounds a bit ridiculous," Clarissa said, "but the same description was given today to the Sheriff."

"How do you know that?" I asked.

"That's... well, let me keep some secrets for now, all right?"

I paused. I didn't like not knowing where someone got their information, but at the same time, I didn't know this woman well enough to ask her to trust us. Not yet.

"All right," I said. "That's fair. But you know for sure that the descriptions match?"

She nodded. "Different witnesses gave the exact same description."

"I'm surprised the perp in question didn't have on a black pointy hat and carry a broom," Gil said.

"It does seem a little weird," I said. "The description."

"I know," Clarissa said. "Add that to the evidence found—"

A strange sound cut through the roar of the surf, interrupting Clarissa. I looked over my shoulder, squinting into the darkness.

It was the sound of wood clacking against rock, a faint *tap... tap... tap...* and the sound was approaching.

"*Something's coming,*" I whispered.

CHAPTER 8. THE ILLUSION

Gil took a breath. "What is–"

"Quiet," I whispered.

There was something else. My eyes were useless, so I closed them, focusing all my attention on the faint sound as it approached.

Tap... tap... tap...

The other sound. It was slow and regular, almost like a deep, raspy breathing, only not quite. It sounded like–

Dragging. It sounded like something sheathed in cloth was being dragged across the rocks.

I opened my eyes, and realized I was holding my breath. I could feel my pulse quickening. I was afraid. Everywhere I looked in the direction of the sound was darkness. Behind me, Clarissa had raised the flashlight, pointing the narrow beam in the direction of the sound.

Tap... tap... tap...

The light was a mere pinprick in the ocean of pitch blackness that seemed to be closing in on us.

Beside me, Gil began muttering something under his breath. I recognized the words as his incantations. He was focusing his energy.

In a moment, a faint orange flame engulfed his

right fist, casting a low flickering light across the pavement. The glow only extended a few feet before it was swallowed in the gloom.

I tapped the vael, releasing a flood of energy as my own fist exploded in a wreath of blue-white fire, much brighter and more powerful than Gil's. The fire trick was pretty much the only thing I'd mastered.

"What is that?" Clarissa asked, her voice low. "And was that... fire that just shot from your–?"

"*Shhh*," I urged.

Tap... tap... tap...

"I don't know what it is," Gil whispered.

"It's definitely getting closer."

"Where's Finch?"

"I don't know, but that's not him."

"I'm frightened," Clarissa said, her voice fluttery as she drew quick breaths. "What's happening?"

The beam of her light flashed across the wide expanse of nothing, but I couldn't help but follow it's pale white glow, hoping beyond hope it would expose something innocent.

I hoped it would, but I knew better.

"Finch?" Gil called softly. "Finch?"

A new sound came from the dark, a *clack clack clack clack* that was unmistakably teeth chattering, a jaw opening and closing repeatedly.

"Hecate, give us strength," Clarissa moaned. Her flashlight whipped through the darkness as the *tap tap tap* grew nearer.

"Dylan," Gil said. "Gimme some more light, eh

big man?"

I pushed more power into my hand, the blue-white light growing in intensity, pushing the sphere of light farther into the darkness. Still, we saw nothing.

The *tap tap tap* continued, closer and closer.

"Where the hell is that coming from?" Gil asked, turning to look behind us.

And then it stopped.

For a long moment, there was silence.

Clarissa took a sharp inhale of breath, her light shaking in her hands.

Somewhere above, a seagull called.

Distracted, I looked up, and I almost missed it. Ahead of us, a black robe flashed in the darkness, slicing through Clarissa's light like a knife. She screamed.

"What the hell?" Gil shouted. He stepped backwards and tripped over the sandbags. "WHOA!"

In the darkness, the *clack clack clack* roared to life, practically in my ear. It was just beside me. Clarissa was still screaming as I turned, the pale glow of light shining over a tall, gaunt body wrapped in black.

The vael exploded in my chest, forcing red hot fire out through both of my hands. I tried to aim, but I felt like I was moving in slow motion. The woman in black swung a long, wooden cane and whipped me across the face. Stars exploded in my head as I tumbled backwards, sending columns of flames into the sky like a hellish beacon.

Gil was shouting as he leapt over me, his arms

swinging blindly in the darkness towards the shape. I felt blood on my face as I struggled to sit up. Somewhere nearby, the dune grass was on fire.

Gil crashed into the figure in black, and together they toppled over the rocky edge of the bluff leading back down towards the swampy marsh below.

I pulled myself upright. "Finch!" I shouted. "Where the hell are you?"

"Here!" a voice called from the darkness to my left. "What's wrong?"

"Can't you hear that goddamned screaming? Didn't you see the fire?"

"I found something–"

"I don't give a shit if you found Jimmy Hoffa drinking out of the Holy Grail, get your ass up here!"

Without another lost second, I jumped off the plateau, immediately hitting a rocky hill, and rolled head over feet down towards the glades.

Over jagged edges I rolled, losing any sense of direction, until I hit the ground, caroming off a huge rock semi-submerged in mud. I was really bleeding now.

"Gil?" I asked, dazed. "Boss, are you all right?"

"Ugghhh," I heard a voice grumble from a few feet away. Cautiously, I pushed a little power into my hand, sending a weak beam of light forward.

Gil lay in a pile of crushed cattails, his eyes at half-mast. He looked just like I felt.

"Boss," I said, moving slowly to his side. "Are you all right?"

He sat up, blood running freely from a cut

beneath his eye. "Damn," he moaned. "That wasn't any fun."

"Where's the thing?" I asked. "The woman in black?"

Gil's eyes sharpened and he cast a glance over one shoulder, then the other. "I don't know," he said. "Did you see her?"

"Not after you two went over the edge, no."

"After I hit her, we separated. It was pretty much just me goin' ass over teacups down that damned hill. I have no idea where she went."

I lowered the beam of light to the muddy ground. An unmistakable pair of footprints led off into the darkness.

"So, she beat a path of retreat, eh?" Gil laughed victoriously. "We showed that scary witch lady!"

"Oh yeah," I groaned. "We *definitely* got the last laugh this time."

"All right," Gil said. "Not our finest hour, but she was creepy."

"True story," I said. "Here, gimme your hand. Let me get you on your feet."

Slowly, we made our way back up the hill towards where I'd left Clarissa. When we got there, we found Finch standing at her side, doing his best to comfort her.

"Whatever you saw is now gone," he said callously. "I do not understand why you are frightened. Stop crying."

"Thank you, Finch," I said. "I think you've done quite enough."

"What?" he asked.

"Where the hell were you?"

"Yeah!" Gil said. "I got cut!" he pointed dramatically at the bloody slit beneath his eye. "Where were you!?"

"I am very sorry for that, Boss," Finch said. "I was distracted. I... well, I sensed something and followed it. I got lucky in the darkness."

"You gonna show us?" Gil asked.

"Absolutely."

As he and Finch shuffled off in the darkness, I took Clarissa's hand and helped her to her feet.

"That was... I'm sorry to say, quite terrifying," she said, sounding ashamed.

"No need to be embarrassed," I said. "It really scared the shit out of me, honestly."

She laughed. "I'm quite relieved to hear that, young man."

"Shall we?" I gestured towards where Gil and Finch had gone.

"Yes, I believe we should."

Together, we followed the sound of my associates' voices, moving away from the artillery at the hilltop and towards the ocean. At some point, we began descending the other side of the hill, about halfway down, we found Finch and Gil studying a lichen-covered rock face.

"Glad you could make it, big man," Gil said. "And Madame," he smiled cordially to Clarissa. "What do you think of this?" he asked with a flourish.

There, carved into the rock face, was a pairing of

symbols. The first was a pair of interlocked circles. The second a long vertical line with two shorter perpendicular intersecting lines, one near the top and one near the bottom.

"Good gracious," Clarissa said. "Those are runes." She turned to us, her eyes wide. "Witches' Runes."

CHAPTER 9. THE ENTERTAINING OF A SHY GIRL

Gil was singing off key as Clarissa applied butterfly stitches to the minute cut beneath his eye. He'd insisted on the butterfly stitches because he said they'd make him look "tough."

"*I can't stop this feelin', deep inside of meeee... girl you just don't realize what you do to meeee...*"

"Are you trying to tell me something, Mr. Abercrombie?" Clarissa asked, smiling.

"*When you hold me... in your arms so tight, you let me know... everything's all right...*"

"No," Finch said, slowly turning a page in a book he was reading at her desk. "He is always like this."

"*I'm... hooked on a–!*"

"Mr. Abercrombie?" Clarissa asked.

"Don't call me that, girl!" he said, nodding his head in time to the Blue Swede beat he could probably hear in his head. "And do you have any wine? Because... *you've got me thirsting–*"

"You don't drink wine," I said as I finished applying a bandaid to my forehead. "You're more a fruit drink type. You know, piña coladas, daquiris, dark and stormys–"

"Oh you're missin' a *huge* one," Gil said. "Hello? Mai Tais?"

"Of course," I said, shutting off the bathroom light. "Silly me."

"Hey Madame C, don't call me Mr. Abercrombie, please," Gil said as Clarissa stood back to survey her work. "Nobody calls me that. Just make it Gil."

"Then you can call me Clarissa," she turned to me. "That goes for all of you, please."

"That's just plain Finch, and that guy's still just Dylan," Gil said. "We're pretty casual."

"No one calls me Madame Clarissa," our host said, taking a seat in an easy chair and yawning. "Not even the occasional legitimate client I'm lucky enough to land."

"You must do all right," Gil said, looking around her house. "You live in a pretty sweet place!"

He wasn't wrong. The boring waiting room and tacky "office" downstairs gave no hint as to the understated comfort that lay on the second floor. The house was small but clean and well-kept, and there was obvious love put into the small things: the watercolor hanging in the kitchen, the family pictures on every table, the dog bed beneath the kitchen table– and accompanying Corgi named Jonathan, the bookcases in place of a television, the knitting needles and yarn beneath the coffee table. And there were books on nearly every surface, everything from Rita Mae Brown to Fyodor Dostoevsky. Some houses are well lived-in and well-loved, and this small cottage was one such house.

"Thank you," Clarissa said. "I like it. Are you

sure I can't get you anything to drink?" she asked for at least the third time.

"No, thank you," Gil and I said simultaneously. Finch simply shook his head.

It got quiet, and I found myself reading the titles on her bookshelf. I saw more than a few novels that I'd read myself, making me like our host even more. A few minutes ticked by in silence; perhaps everyone felt as lost for words as I did–and as tired. There's usually an awkward period after something strange and unsettling happens; added to the fact that we were in a stranger's house and things were bound to move slowly at first.

"Did the witches take the children?" Clarissa asked suddenly.

"Okay, so we're cuttin' right to it, eh?" Gil asked, scratching his shaggy hair as Jonathan the Corgi began sniffing his foot.

"I... well, the thought had already occurred to me," she said. "Honestly, it's been bothering me for a while." She looked at her slippered feet. "You know what could have happened...?"

Finch looked up from the thick book on the desktop. "What?"

Clarissa stood and crossed the cozy den, making her way towards the small kitchen that overlooked the backyard. "I'm going to make some tea, I think. Can I interest anyone in a cup."

Gil and I declined. Finch on the other hand, accepted gratefully.

"But wait. What could have happened?" Gil

asked.

From the kitchen, I heard the *clang* of the tea kettle and the rush of water from the tap. In a moment, Clarissa returned to the den.

"I told you," she said. "I tried to join their coven. I wanted so much to be a part of it. I'd never shared this with anyone," she said. "I've never known another Wiccan. I've never felt a part of something larger than myself, and that is one of the core principles of Wicca."

"I thought it was being one with the Earth and not eating meat or cheese and stuff," Gil ventured.

"Well, that's... complicated," Clarissa said, leaning back. "Wicca is complicated because it's so splintered. Many people practice, sharing a range of beliefs, but unlike Christianity, there is really no central dogma, so unfortunately a great deal of practitioners pick and choose what they believe and how they practice. There are so many different traditions of Wicca it is a little overwhelming."

"All right, so you tried to join their coven–"

Clarissa nodded, cutting Gil off. "I tried," she said. "It was hard enough to learn who they were. I only found them by staking out a local occult shop until I found someone purchasing things I recognized."

"What happened next?"

"I..." She trailed off, and a blush crept into her cheeks. "Well, I introduced myself and asked how long she'd been practicing." Clarissa took a deep breath, the blush on her face darkening. "She... well, let's just say it didn't go well. She recognized me and had a number of... *unkind* things to say to me. Apparently she didn't think my chosen profession cast a good light on the Wicca community."

Gil was frowning. "And so that was that?"

Clarissa nodded. "That was that," she said. In the kitchen, her tea pot began to screech. She stood and walked to it.

"This woman in question seems quite unpleasant," Finch said. "Perhaps we should pay her a visit, Boss."

"I agree," Gil said.

So did I, but I didn't need to say it. I simply nodded.

When Clarissa returned, she had two mugs of tea on a tray beside a beer and a glass of chocolate milk. In the center of the tray was a small, round coffee cake.

"I guessed," Clarissa said, setting the tray down on the center table and passing out drinks. "How did I do?"

Gil got the chocolate milk, I got the beer, and Finch got the tea.

"You hit that nail right on the head, sweetheart!" Gil said, laughing. "It's like you've known us for years.

She smiled. "Here, take a plate." She passed out a few small desert plates, forks, and paper napkins, cartoon bears adorning them. I didn't care it was almost dawn, I was going to wreck that cake.

"All right," Gil said, chewing. "So you met this bitchy lady and she was bitchy. What happened next?"

Clarissa wiped her mouth with a napkin and shook her head. "Nothing else, really. Although it wasn't long after that Benji was kidnapped."

"And you think they are involved?" Gil asked.

"I didn't at first," she shook her head and took a sip of tea. "Not at first. But I heard the eyewitness statement, and it made me think. Then there was the evidence found at the hotel–"

"Hold on," I said, putting down my plate. "What evidence?"

"I told you about it at–wait, no, we were interrupted by that... well. Um, there was evidence found at the scene of the first kidnapping. A little information about it was released, but there was nothing found at the second crime scene. That's why I was going to see it tonight."

"What was found at the first scene?"

"I'll show you," she said, standing. She walked to the bookshelf and dug through a few hardback titles, finally pulling a thick old tome free. Carefully, she laid it down on the long coffee table beside the coffee cake and opened it, flipping through pages.

"This," she said, pointing. Gil and I leaned in. Finch put down his tea cup and came over for a look.

Inside the old book was a faded black and white image of a round pendant marked with a six-sided star and encircled in some kind of markings.

"That's not an exact match," she said. "But I spoke with one of the witnesses and they said it looked just like it."

"What are these markings?" Gil asked, pointing

at the strange rune-looking shapes.

"Those are characters," Finch said. "Hebrew characters."

"Yes, exactly," Clarissa said. "It's a Solomon Amulet for protection."

"Solomon?" I asked.

"King Solomon," Finch said. "King of Israel, son of David? This star is generally known as the Star of David, but it first appeared in medieval Kabbalistic texts, described as the Seal of Solomon."

I groaned, I couldn't help it. When Finch put on his Professor voice, I had a hard time sticking with it. He continued:

"History and legend say that Solomon held dominion over spirits and demons through a ring that bore this symbol." He looked at us. "Am I the only one who reads?"

Gil stared at Finch blankly. After a long moment, he nodded.

"I read... novels," I said, a tad defensively.

Finch sighed.

"You're *exactly* right about all of it!" Clarissa laughed. "Brilliant! It's so good to speak with someone who knows these things!"

"And so because of the Seal of Solomon, you assumed Wiccan involvement?" Finch asked.

"Yes, I did. I don't know any other reason this would be found at the scene."

"It could have been planted," I suggested.

"I don't know how may people are familiar with the Seal of Solomon. And what about the eyewitness account?" she asked. "That description–"

Gil shook his head. "If you're gonna say 'looks like a witch,' you better look in the mirror, kiddo. You don't 'look like a witch,' and you *are* a witch."

"All right, that's fair. But what about the runes tonight?"

"That is precisely what I was researching in your book," Finch said. "I hope you do not mind." He gestured to the open book that sat on her desk. "I saw this on your desk."

"Not at all. I recognize runes, but... but I've never had the time to study them in depth."

Finch retrieved the book. "Well, here they are," he said, handing it over.

On the spread pages were a number of symbols–thirteen in all. Finch pointed.

"The first we saw are the rings, a symbol of coming together, a contract, or association. The second," he pointed to the vertical line cut by two perpendicular intersects, "is called the black rune, sometimes drawn as a scythe."

"The black rune, eh?" Gil asked. "I bet that's something great, like symbolizing peace and happiness and free pudding and Netflix for every-body."

"Not quite," Finch said. "The black rune means that a negative force will have an adverse effect on you."

"Ah, yeah," Gil sighed. "I'm not surprised."

"And so in tandem?" I asked.

"Well, that is open for interpretation," Finch said.

"You see, runes should always be taken together, as they are believed to effect one another, but I am certainly no expert."

"But what do you think?"

Finch sighed. "I believe these two runes imply that the maker is uniting with another for... illicit ends."

"That's putting it mildly," I said, shaking my head.

"So you mean one bad thing is gonna hook up with another bad thing and do worse things together?" Gil said.

"Yes, I believe I mean just that," Finch said.

"I bet you're regretting getting involved with this, aren't you?" I asked Clarissa.

She smiled, a little ruefully, perhaps, and said, "Not a bit."

Gil began to tell Clarissa a story about something, and I found myself studying the pictures on the walls, bookshelves, and tables. They were all at least a few years old. Clarissa was in most, and the silver that had crept into her hair was not yet present in the pictures. What *was* present in the pictures was a smiling chubby man with a bushy brown mustache and thinning hair. In many of the pictures, including a batch from Disney World, he held her hand. In others, he had a long arm wrapped around her shoulders. The most recent picture looked to be about ten years old or so. As Clarissa laughed at one of Gil's jokes, I looked at her hands and saw a simple wedding band on her left ring finger.

"You know," Clarissa said, "I never asked who you are."

"You know, I was wonderin' about that, Clarissa," Gil said. "You don't know us at all; you need to be more careful who you invite back to your sweet bachelor*ette* pad!"

"Well, I got a brief glimpse into Dylan there," she said, nodding in my direction, "and I could tell you were good people. I just knew it. I knew I could trust you. What I don't know is *who* you are. Really."

Gil stood up quickly, dropping his fork. "We're *heroes*, that's who! Golly."

"Sort of," I said.

"Hardly," Finch said, turning a page.

"No, no no, don't listen to them," Gil said. "We try to do good things for people. Try and help, you know? So when we heard about what was happenin' here–"

"We were on vacation, actually," I said.

"Yeah, we were," Gil said. "But that doesn't matter. We can still bust punks like nobody's business." He smiled and struck his hero pose. "Superman or Green Lantern ain't got nothin' on me!"

"Oh my," Clarissa laughed.

"Seriously," I said, "you do need to be more careful. Especially if this keeps escalating. We *were* just attacked at Fort Miles, remember."

"I know. I... I've never had anything like that ever happen to me," she said, shaking her head. "It was truly frightening."

"It's all right now," Gil said. "We're on it. We

Zeros are gonna find this witch or whatever and shut her down! Welcome to jail, witchy woman!"

"Zeros?" Clarissa asked, taking a sip of her tea.

"It's our name!" Gil said. "Finch picked it out, actually, in a rare moment of creativity."

"I believe it was a not-so-rare moment of extreme pessimism," Finch said, taking a sip of tea himself.

"Worth nothin' to no one, is what he says, that goon," Gil said, shaking his head. "Ergo Zeros. It's kind of stuck."

"Worth nothing to no one?" Clarissa smiled sadly. "I can tell you one thing: I know for a fact that is not true."

I opened my mouth, trying to find a way to broach the subject of her husband, when she yawned loudly.

"I'm sorry," she said, "I am getting so very tired. And I think I can see the sun beginning to crawl towards the horizon. It will be day before we know it."

"You need your rest!" Gil said. "And we better go! When it's this time of night and I'm not in my jammies, I start gettin' grumpy. We got your card, right?"

Finch stood and nodded. "It's in my wallet," he said.

"And I think we got some kind of portable wire-less phone thing?" Gil said.

"Yes, both Dylan and I have mobile phones, Boss," Finch said.

"Ah, magical!" He stood, crumbs falling off his

shirtfront. "All right, time to hit the bricks!" He turned to us. "Ready, gents?"

We slipped out with little ceremony, waving goodbye and thanking Clarissa for her exposition and hospitality. There was something grateful in the way she smiled at us, but something sad, as well. I liked her. It's hard not to like someone who is so willing to put herself in danger to help innocent children—someone else's children, at that. She made a meager living reading palms, tea leaves, and tarot, and spent her spare time knitting and practicing Wicca. It would seem to the casual observer that she was quite different from us Zeros.

But we knew better. She was one of us.

CHAPTER 10. WIDOW WITH SHAWL (A PORTRAIT)

It was late when I finally got out of bed, and I was pleased to learn that I'd not slept as late as Gil. I showered, shaved, and met Finch in his room, where he sat reading Clarissa's book on runes, dark circles under his eyes.

"Were you up all night?" I asked.

He nodded. "I only sleep when I'm bored," he said. "I am hundreds of years old. I have slept enough."

I tried to make small talk with Finch for a while, but finally ran out of steam. When he is in full research mode, he is totally disinterested in conversation. I can only carry a conversation for so long. I called Gil at one o'clock, waking him from what sounded like a deep sleep. He took another half hour to get dressed and it was nearly two before we arrived at our first meal of the day.

"Good grief," Gil said, hunkering down in a booth in a small Mom and Pop diner a stone's throw from the boardwalk. Finch sat beside him and I slipped in the opposite side.

"I feel hungover," Gil moaned. "When was the last time we pulled an all nighter?"

"Callowleigh," Finch said. "You and Dylan were trapped–"

"Yes, I remember," Gil said. "What's the word? Rhetorical? Is that right?"

"It was twenty-nine days ago–"

"All right, Professor, all right," Gil said. "Rhetorical is *definitely* the word. I've heard you say it enough times in your 'snooty' tone."

"You're gettin' old, Boss," I said, smiling.

He raised a hand, signaling a waitress. "Coffee, please!"

"So are we going to talk about last night?" I asked.

"What would you like to talk about?" Finch responded.

I stared at him for a moment, but he was stone-faced. "Well," I said. "I got this cut here," I pointed at my bandaided face, "and the Boss has that cut there," I said, pointing at Gil's butterfly stitches.

"–and they make me look tough!" he said, gratefully accepting a cup of coffee from the returning waitress.

"Coffee, gentlemen?" she asked, holding the pot in our direction.

"Yes, please," I said.

"Excuse me, madame, but do you have tea?"

"Of course. One tea, coming up." She looked at us. "You guys have a rough night? Been in a fight?"

"You see?" I asked Finch. "She noticed."

The waitress smiled before shuffling off for

Finch's tea.

"I noticed," Finch said. "But after a night like last night, I believe we have a great deal to talk about."

"At the moment I'm most concerned with the scary black-robed thing who bitch-slapped me with her cane."

"I took care of her for you, big man," Gil said, pouring a generous helping of sugar into his already heavily creamed coffee. "Knocked that old lady down that hill like Humpty Dumpty."

"I think you mean Jack and Jill," Finch said. "You're mixing nursery rhymes."

"Yeah, didn't Humpty Dumpty fall off a wall?"

"Speaking of Jack and Jill," Gil said, "do you think they have ice cream here? I didn't want ice cream until you said—"

"*Anyway*," I interrupted. "What happened last night? What attacked us?"

Finch opened his mouth slowly and said, "I..." his mouth closed and he glanced at each of us slowly. "All right," he said, "I don't know what it was."

"My money's definitely on an old lady," Gil said. "I didn't see the fabled nose that Clarissa was referencin', but I felt how skinny and bony she was. Although I'll give it to the old bird, she could move pretty fast."

"She could, I agree," Finch said. "But have you stopped to wonder why she was there?"

"What do you mean?" I asked.

"The immediate thought is that she was there to inscribe the runes on the stone, correct? However, I had already located the runes at the time of the attack."

"So you're thinkin' the old bat didn't draw the pictures?" Gil asked.

"No, certainly not."

"Then who did?"

"That is the question, Boss," Finch said. "I also find it quite strange that only the two of you were accosted by the figure in black."

"Why is that weird?" Gil said.

"Because if you look at the situation on a threat level analysis, neither you nor Dylan were threats," Finch said, thanking our waitress as she returned with his cup of tea. "The witch Clarissa is an obvious threat to the ominous figure in black considering she is also a witch."

Our waitress raised a skeptical eyebrow at Finch's last sentence.

"We'll need another minute," I said, smiling. She turned and tended to an adjacent table.

"That makes sense," Gil said, pouring more sugar in his coffee. "But in that case, why would the witch lady *not* go right for Clarissa?"

"Wait," I said. "I don't much like the direction you're headed."

"Nor do I, Dylan, but do you not find it suspect that the book she had on runes was not on her bookshelf, but sitting *open* on her desk?"

"Well, a little–"

"And did you not find it strange that I found the *exact* runes in the book that I saw at Fort Miles?"

"Like I said, I don't like where this conversation is headed." I leaned back and took a sip of my own coffee, black. Finch had his logic, but this felt... *wrong*. And it was kind of pissing me off.

"But you were a police officer, Dylan," Finch said, frowning. "Would you really not draw these same connections?"

"I..." I took a deep breath and let it out slowly. "I admit, I noticed that the book was open on her desk. I also noticed that she hesitated when she said she didn't know much about runes. Those two facts seem to conflict, I'll give you that. It was also a little peculiar for a practicing Wiccan to say that eyewitness reports 'sounded' like a witch."

"I thought that, too," Gil said, adding more cream to his coffee.

"Then what is the problem?" Finch asked, a not so well-masked look of disapproval on his face.

"My gut," I said. "I trust my gut. And my gut says Clarissa is all right."

Finch smiled. "This morning–while you two slept, I contacted Willa and asked her to look into 'Madame Clarissa.'"

"Why are you using air quotes around 'Madame Clarissa'?" I asked.

"Because her real name is Claire Donnegan," Finch said. "And she is not licensed–"

"Hold on, you don't need a license to be a–" I lowered my voice, "–a *psychic*."

"That is true," Finch said. "But she would need a business license and a permit to operate out of her house, neither of which she has."

"That doesn't say anything," I said, shaking my head. "It just says... she's a little disorganized."

"Well, it might say a *little* teeny bit more than that," Gil said. "It says that she's not *totally* above board, big man." He looked around for our waitress. "Hey, you boys ready to order?" he asked.

"No," Finch and I said in chorus.

"Okay, good." He waved energetically for our waitress. "Ready!" he said.

"You boys all set?" she asked.

"You know it! Okay, I'm gonna have grilled cheese. No, wait. *Two* grilled cheeses. And, this is weird, but can you put scrapple on them?"

"Scrapple?"

"Scrapple, absolutely. The only thing in this world better than bacon is scrapple. I'd put it on ice cream if these guys would let me," he smiled at Finch and I. "Speaking of, do you have ice cream?"

"Sure."

"Okay, cool."

"I will have a western omelette, please," I said. "With hash browns and wheat toast."

"All right. How about you, young man?"

"Who? Oh, me," Finch said, smiling. "I'll have a salad please. And a cup of whatever soup you have today."

"Clam chowder," she said, scribbling on her pad. She took our menus with a nod. "It'll be right up."

"Okay," I said. "Where were we?"

"Clarissa's not 100% kosher," Gil said. "Etc, etc, etc."

"Ah, yeah, what about—"

"There is another thing Willa found," Finch said.

"What is that?"

"Claire Donnegan was married to a Stuart Donnegan for fourteen years until his death two years ago in Washington, DC. It was reported as an accident, but Willa's research did show that the police opened an investigation into his death, citing possible foul play. Claire—or Clarissa—was a suspect."

"Of course she'd be a suspect," I growled, something angry beginning to wake up inside me. "The spouse is *always* a suspect at first. Were any charges ultimately filed?"

"No. The death was deemed accidental."

"Then that should tell you a lot. It should tell you that Clarissa was involved in some tragic stuff in Washington, DC and moved here to start a new life. Whatever evil straws you're grasping for, stop."

Gil cleared his throat. "Are you thinkin' straight here? I liked her too, big man, but these are some not-so-great things. I got a gut feeling, too, and it's good, so don't worry, but we need to put this stuff in our back pocket and not forget about it."

"Back pocket is fine," I said, "but I refuse to believe that she is involved in this mess."

"She's definitely involved," Finch said. "At the moment, she is merely involved on our side of it."

"You know what I mean," I grumbled.

The conversation died out, and we all tended to

our respective coffee or tea. I remembered noticing Clarissa's wedding ring last night, and I'd really hoped I'd been wrong. Turns out I wasn't. The man in the photographs with the bushy mustache must have been her husband. Her sadness made infinitely more sense. So did her desire to be part of a group, and the depression that followed her rejection. Her house suddenly seemed a little smaller and a little less comfortable. A cozy home had become a hideaway for a woman who was looking for a place to regroup and start again. Learning more about Clarissa had not changed how I felt about her, but it lent a much better perspective to everything I'd seen and heard.

Our food arrived and we dug in. Halfway through, I noticed Gil smiling over my shoulder and waving. I turned around and saw the young boy Gil had taught to fly kites on the beach. He smiled and waved back.

"You better watch out," I said. "You're gonna get us arrested again."

"No, I'm not," he said. "I'm just bein' nice."

"A lot of people frown on old men 'being nice' to young boys," I said.

"That's messed up, man!" Gil said, dropping his sandwich. "I was just bein' nice! Like normal nice!"

"Well, you better watch out anyway," I said, nodding towards the door. "We're not on the best terms with the local PD, remember?"

Gil turned to see Sheriff Huggins stride into the small diner. He walked slowly to the front counter and accepted a to-go bag from our waitress. He paid in cash, and as he was turning to leave, he noticed us. He frowned. Gil waved and the Sheriff frowned further.

"Boss..." I cautioned.

"I'm still just bein' nice! What's so wrong with bein' nice?"

The Sheriff gave us an honest to God *I'm-watching-you* gesture before turning and leaving, sparing one last glance at us before walking out the door.

"Friendly town," Gil said, shaking his head. "You'd think that guy would thank us!"

"For starting a fight on the beach in the height of the summer? Yeah right."

"We weren't starting–"

"Before we get derailed again," I said, putting down my fork. "Can we just jump back for one more second?"

"To what?" Gil asked.

Finch looked up from his soup, frowning characteristically.

"The thing in black," I said. "What was it?"

"You mean, are we really thinking it's a witch?" Gil asked.

"Yeah, that's what I want to know."

We both looked at Finch.

"I don't have access to any of my books," he said, "and this would frankly be easier if we were back at the office–"

"Yeah, yeah, yeah," Gil said. "Cut to your verdict, old man. I've been on the fence since I tack-led the weird sister last night."

Finch sighed. "Remember, I did not see this figure in black. But from what I have heard, I do not believe it to be a witch. Too many things are failing to add up."

"Unfortunately," Gil said. "I agree."

"Where does that leave us?" I asked.

Gil shrugged. "We have to start asking questions. You know, doin' that investigation thing." He checked his watch. "I need to make a call, and then we gotta run. There's someone you and I need to meet," Gil said, elbowing Finch.

"What about me?"

"I want you to check out the hotel where the first kid was snatched. See if you can find the witness. Talk to people. Look around. Snoop. You know, be a cop."

"I'm not a cop."

"Not anymore. But you know *how* to be a cop."

"Okay."

Gil dropped a few twenties on the table. "Let's go."

We stood and walked towards the door, Gil leading the way. Outside, I could see that traffic was already heavy, no surprise considering most vacationers had been on the beach for 4+ hours already.

Gil looked back over his shoulder. "Maybe if we get done early we can finally play some skee–"

He stopped as he bumped into someone in the doorway.

"Oh, excuse me I–"

"*YOU.*"

"Aw, it's *you*."

I looked over Finch's shoulder. Our nemesis Ponytail stood in the doorway. He wore a cut off New York Giants tee shirt and purple bathing suit. He slipped a pair of reflective sunglasses up his nose with one hand and pointed at Gil with his other.

"Watch where you're going, hippie," he said.

"Hippie?" Gil asked, genuinely confused.

"Yeah! Get a haircut or something. And get a job while you're at it!"

"What?"

"Come on, Don," a petite woman said from behind him. "Let's just sit down."

"We will, Charlene," Ponytail said. "I just want this goon to know who's boss."

"If you like," Gil said, "I'll have my buddy give you some boxing lessons again. You were a quick study last time!"

Ponytail frowned and shook his head. "Buncha weirdos," he said, walking past. The slight woman Charlene–I assume his wife–followed. At her heels was a chubby young girl with pigtails.

"Love the shirt, kiddo," Gil said, nodding at her Wonder Woman tee shirt. He gave her a high five before slipping out the door behind her.

Outside, Gil took the keys to the Tank. "I think I'll drive," he told me. "I have a feeling our errand will only take a minute. Then we'll swing back and get you."

"Where are you going again?" I asked.

"That shall remain a secret." He smiled broadly.

"You will just have to wait and see. Now let's get moving. We got crimes to solve and a schedule to keep." He glanced at his watch again. "Funland opens in two hours, my friends, and I plan on being there when they do." He looked at us. "We three have a date with the skee-ball lanes. Now, let's roll!"

CHAPTER 11. AS I RECALL IT

I'd not ridden with Gil often, and each time I did, I swore I'd never do it again. Between his fiddling with the radio, pointing out "neat" restaurants, and honking at other drivers, he barely had time to steer. After about eight close calls, he let me out at a hotel on the Lewes strip, a spitting distance from Midway.

"We'll come getcha," he said from his open window. "Just be cool until then."

"It's 97° out here. How long am I gonna have to 'just be cool'?" I asked.

"I dunno, big dog. 'Til we're done? Like I said, this should only take a minute. Or ten. We'll call, okay?"

"All right," I said. "But try and keep it quick. I'm not used to being without the car." Honestly, the idea of waiting on Gil was less than rosy. He had a rather casual relationship with time.

"If we're late, just hang out there!" he pointed at a small tropical-themed water park called Kokomo Joe's snugged in beside the hotel parking lot where I stood.

"Oh yeah, I'll definitely be doing that," I said sarcastically.

"Okay! Good!" He waved a few times and

puttered off, a salvo of honking heralding his re-entry into traffic.

Not far from the Midway, the busy strip of Lewes was chock-full of chain restaurants, outlet malls, surf shops, and resort-related businesses–like the aforementioned water park, a varied selection of mini-golf courses, go karts, and sea shell shops. With this in mind, you can imagine the menagerie of beach-themed hotels, motels, and motor-lodges that mixed in, completing the vacation community aesthetic. Most of them were those U-shaped one or two story jobs with outdoor entrances that looked like they were designed in about 1975. Gil would have been pleased with the cheesy names, too. Breezy Sea Motel, Conch Cove Motor Lodge, Rehoboth Beach Dreams, as well as more creative ones like the Ocean Motel. It was in the latter's parking lot that I stood just now.

The Ocean Motel was as unremarkable as it sounded. A pair of white, narrow, red-roofed buildings ran parallel on either side of a wide parking lot. In the center of the parking lot sat the manager's office and a kidney bean-shaped pool. A *NO VACANCY* sign blinked in the office window.

I crossed the cramped for a parking lot, a baking desert in the hot June sun. The swimming pool had a decidedly yellow hue to it, something I hoped was due to the almost neon sun that poured down on it. A skinny tan woman in a bikini was sleeping face down on a lounge chair while a pair of kids splashed around in the pool. I opened the door to the office, and a bell overhead rang.

Inside, it was hot and sticky. A rotating fan was

humming on a long, empty counter, and an AC window unit rattled ineffectually from the back corner. As the door closed behind me, a tall, lanky man emerged from the back room, wiping sweat from his face with a handkerchief. He wore small round glasses and a pencil-thin mustache.

"Can I help you?" he asked.

"Got any rooms available?" I asked.

He nodded at the *NO VACANCY* sign. "Sorry, friend," he said. "It's a tough time of year for walk-ins. You can try the Ruby Sandcastle up on the John J. Williams Highway, but they had bedbugs, so buyer beware."

"I was more interested in this place," I said, casually flipping through some fliers on a rack by the door. The first one I grabbed was for the tropical-themed water park in the next lot. "The kids like the water park and the wife likes the pool." I slipped my wedding ring-bereft left hand into my pocket.

The man smiled and slipped his handkerchief into his breast pocket. "The park is a nice draw," he said. "We get a lot of families here."

"You the manager?" I asked.

His eyes narrowed slightly, the barest hint of suspicion showing through. "Yes," he said. "The name's Raleigh, Fred Raleigh."

"Owner too?"

He nodded. "Bought it about six years ago. I've worked just about every day since that first day."

I nodded and grabbed another flier off the rack. This one was for a Viking-themed mini golf course in

Fenwick.

"You have a hard time with the cops when that kid got taken?"

"Excuse me?"

"Benjamin Mason, Jr.," I said. "I imagine you were grilled pretty hard over that one."

"Now see here–"

"Relax," I said, "I like your place here, I'm just a little worried about the safety of my kids, that's all."

"My establishment is *very* safe," he said. "Now maybe you should–"

"Were you here when it happened?"

"I..." Raleigh trailed off. "I told you already, I've worked just about every day we been open here since I bought the place."

"Six years ago."

"Yeah, that's right, six years ago."

"So you were here."

"I... yeah, I was here." He retrieved the hand-kerchief from his pocket and wiped his face again just as a bead of sweat trickled down his temple.

"What happened, Mr. Raleigh?"

"I'd rather not–"

"I'm helping the family," I lied. "I'm just asking some questions."

He squinted at me. There was that suspicion again.

"I already talked to Sheriff Hanley," he said. "I told them everything."

"Hanley...?" I asked. After a moment it occurred

to me. "The Sheriff of Lewes."

"Yeah. The Sheriff and a his deputy, some woman named McCauley. They got my statement the day it happened."

"Why don't you tell me?"

"I already told–"

"Tell me," I repeated.

He swallowed, looking over my shoulder out at the parking lot. I glanced back and saw a cop car coast by.

"Looks like they're still watching you," I said. "Maybe they're not so sure this place is safe."

"It *is*," he said, a hint of desperation in his voice. "I run a good clean business here, buddy. Family-friendly, you know?"

"Relax, all I want to know is what happened. What did you see?"

The handkerchief was back. It was hot in the office, even with the fan, but was it that hot?

He swallowed and took a deep breath. Then, his voice low, he said, "*A witch.*"

"A witch?"

He nodded. "I was in here, settling the books for the day before. It was four in the afternoon or so and busy because people were coming back from the beach. There were a lot of cars outside."

"Okay."

"I'm sitting here," he gestured at the tall chair beside him, "adding up receipts when this big van of kids pulls up. College kids on vacation."

"All right."

"The van blocks the window, see?" he pointed. The office had big windows on three of the walls, one facing each strip of the hotel and one facing Route 1. "They parked illegally there, blocking that window, so I went outside to tell 'em to move it. I told 'em, 'you can't park that thing there!' See, I gotta be able to see all the rooms."

"What happened next?"

"Some kid starts giving me lip about it's just for a second and then he's walking away. I wasn't done talking, so I started goin' after him. That's when I saw her."

"The witch?"

He nodded and took a deep breath. "Tall, skinny woman back by #7."

"Where is #7?" I asked.

Raleigh walked out from behind the counter and moved quickly to the window. "Over there," he said, pointing. "Over in the corner there is #7, you see?"

From where we stood, I could see that the #7 room was the last in the row of rooms, beyond which laid what looked like an alley.

"Okay, so you see a figure in black–"

"It was a *woman*," he said, his voice raspy. "Tall and skinny with a long, pointy nose. It was a witch, I tell you."

"Dressed in black?"

"Yeah, dressed in black. Stick thin, too. Like *thin*, thin."

"Okay I got that, she was skinny. What else did

you see?"

"I saw the kid bein' dragged towards the back, over there."

"What's back there?"

"Additional parking, a couple dumpsters, and the laundry room."

"What did you do next?"

He swallowed again, and the handkerchief was wiping more sweat from his face. "I stopped talkin' to the college kid and went after the witch."

"And?"

"And she got around the corner of #7 before I could. I finally got back there and it's empty."

"Is there a back entrance?"

He nodded. "Leads back to Bay Crossing which'll take you down to the Coastal Highway again."

"What did you do next?"

"I called the Lewes Police, of course! What do you think I did? I'd just seen a damned witch taking a kid!"

"What else did you tell them?"

He took a breath and held it. "What do you mean?" he asked finally.

"What else did you tell the Lewes Sheriff that you're not telling me?"

"That's it!"

I watched him, waiting. There was something else, I could feel it. I'd questioned suspects and witnesses enough to learn ticks and habits people have when they withhold information or lie. There was something he wasn't telling me.

"Nothing about what you saw? Nothing about where you were or who else was here?"

"No, that's it, man."

I waited, but he just stared at me, breathing heavily and sweating.

Behind us, the door opened and the bell rang, breaking Raleigh's silence. He turned away from me quickly.

"How can I help you?"

The tan woman in the bikini from the pool had sauntered in, barefoot and holding a pack of Marlboro Lights. "Why ain't you turned on the radio, Freddy?"

"Mrs. Cleary–what?" Raleigh was a bit shaken. He licked his lips and cocked his head at her, confused.

"The radio, Freddy," she said, gesturing vaguely into the air. "You didn't turn the radio on today. All I hear out there is those kids shouting!"

"Oh," Raleigh said, coming out of his trance. "Oh. I'm sorry. Oldies all right, Mrs. Cleary?"

"Wouldn't want any of that top 40s crap, would I?"

Raleigh bent below the counter and flipped a switch. Above, a small speaker crackled to life, piping The Chordettes' "Mr. Sandman" into the hot office, mid-chorus.

"How's that?" Raleigh asked.

"Perfect. That music helps me relax," the woman said.

"You know," Raleigh said, completely ignoring my presence, "I remember back when I was in high school—"

I turned and left, the bell *ding*ing as I walked out into the sun again.

CHAPTER 12. OH GOSH

The door closed behind me, and I listened to the Chordettes continue on with "Mr. Sandman." Through the closed door, I could hear Raleigh and Mrs. Cleary going on about times gone by. I checked my watch. I'd only been there for a few minutes; Gil and Finch had probably yet to arrive at their destination. I looked up at the sun and felt every degree of the 97° raining down on me. With who knows how long to wait, I decided to give my years of investigative experience a bit of a work out.

I left the oasis of the manager's office, walking past the pool and across the blacktop towards #7, Ocean Hotel. The kids were still playing in the pool, albeit without Mrs. Cleary's lax supervision. The only proof that she'd been there was the half-full ashtray beside the lounge chair.

The parking lot was a little less than half-full, not surprising for the time of day. From the Ocean Hotel's location on Route 1, even the closest public beach was a 10-15 minute drive away, which ex-plained the 4PM busy rush of returning beach-goers Raleigh had described earlier when Benjamin Mason was kidnapped. On a hot and sunny day such as this, I'd expect nearly every resident of the Ocean Hotel to be on the beach.

A car slowed to let me pass, and I trotted the remaining distance across the lot to the bank of rooms numbered 1-7. The first door was open, with a maid's cleaning cart outside. From the shadowy room I could hear the sound of a vacuum running. I walked past, listening to the constant rush of traffic behind me on Route 1.

The door to #5 opened, and a short, burly man emerged, scowling. He looked up at me and his frown increased.

"Hi," I said.

"Mughhh," he said–or something thereabouts.

"Have you been staying here for long?" I asked as he started past.

He did not respond, nor did he slow. Instead, he continued on, head down, ignoring me.

"Have a great day," I said. Clearly, I had lost none of my remarkable investigative prowess.

At the end of the bank of rooms, room #7 waited. I glanced over my shoulder to see the burly angry guy get into a pickup and rumble away. Other than that, there was no one in sight. I tried the door.

It was locked. I knocked twice. No one answered.

All right, so I mentioned that I was on the force. Yes, this is true, but I was not a detective. Was I prepared to break into a stranger's room looking for clues? Was I even qualified to "look for clues"? Unfortunately, I'm the brawn, remember? I'm not stupid, but frankly I'm better at breaking stuff. "Evidence" for me has to be pretty obvious.

I walked past room #7 and turned the corner, entering the unpaved back alley from which little Ben Mason had been taken. A pair of dumpsters were on my right, a line of air conditioners on my left, each of them humming maniacally in the June heat. I walked the length of the building, my work boots crunching on the rocky ground, moving behind each room, seeing nothing of note except small, opaque bathroom windows. At the end, I turned around and walked back.

The dumpsters were similarly exciting. A recent batch of something fresh gave the dumpster a wet, piquant diaper stink. I walked past them and began crossing a second parking lot, smaller than the first and sequestered from the main lot by a tall white fence.

Around a second, smaller dumpster–this one for recycling–was a small brick building, tucked just behind the fence, a door in its side open. I stopped in front of it and was assailed by the hot smell of fresh laundry. A young man was inside, pulling wads of wet clothing from the washer and stuffing them into an adjacent dryer. He looked up when I stopped in the door, casting a shadow across him.

"Yeah?" he asked.

I walked on. Friendly sort, these Ocean Hotel people.

I got to the end of the laundry building, feeling rather silly. I had a good chance of getting picked up by the cops for loitering if I kept creeping around like I was. I turned around, ready to head out to find a bench near the parking lot when I saw something on the brick of the laundry building.

It was drawn in blue chalk with an unsteady hand, but the image was unmistakable. It was an eye, wide and almond-shaped with a circular pupil in the center. Above was the curved line of an eyelid. Above that and again below the eye were lines of eyelashes.

I'm from Philly; I'd seen my share of graffiti, both good and bad. This was not graffiti. It's hard to describe, but there was a purpose behind it. It wasn't profanity or a hastily drawn private body part, and it lacked the certain panache evident in most graffiti. This was different.

From my pocket, I pulled my phone. It was old, a far cry from the smart phones everybody else had, but it still had a camera. Carefully, I framed the whole image and snapped the picture. Drawn in chalk as it was, I tried to remember if it had rained recently, and I was about six days into my weather recollection when I heard a noise to my right.

I turned, expecting to see the rude kid coming out of the laundry room. Instead, I saw a nebulous black shape slink past. I pocketed my phone, feeling my pulse pick up as I followed.

I tried to focus over the smell of the dumpsters and the rumble of the traffic from Route 1, and it was hard. Slinking after the shape from the laundry room, I tried to tap into the vael, hoping to send out some kind of otherworld radar to give me an idea of what kind of powers I was looking at.

Slipping past the first dumpster, the shape was gone. I continued forward, rounding the second dumpster and saw the flash of black again. The shape was thin and quick, traveling low to the ground in a definite feline posture, forcing me to pick up my pace for fear of losing it.

My vael radar Spidey Sense was picking up nothing, but it didn't stop me from trying. I'd done some minor training with Gil and Finch, and generally I could pick up even the faintest blip from each of them—as Finch explained it, I was reading their own "magical signature." Did that mean this figure in black had no use of magic? *But it's a witch, isn't it?* I wondered.

The shape whipped around the corner of #7, disappearing down the long passage behind the bank of rooms. At the very last moment, the briefest of glances was turned back in my direction.

"Shit," I said.

Spotted, I took off, dropping any pretense of stealth as I raced after the witch. Ahead of me, I could hear light steps barely disturbing gravel as my prey escaped. I tromped after it with all the grace of a charging rhino. Turning the corner, I saw the figure in black screech to a halt at the end of the bank of rooms as a Rehoboth police cruiser came to a stop in the parking lot just off Route 1.

Turning to her right, the thin shape leapt onto a nine-foot tall crimson wooden fence, skittering up and over it in a second. I followed. You'd think my height would give me an advantage; it didn't. It took me two tries to get up and over it, finally tumbling off the back side and landing spread eagle on wet pavement.

I was in Kokomo Joe's water park, at the edge of a narrow wave pool. Kids were everywhere, screaming and splashing in brightly colored swimsuits. More than a couple were pointing at me and my quarry–in a bad way. Thankfully, the figure in black stuck out even more than I did. From where I stood, I could see the mysterious figure's thin shape tearing around the pool, making her way towards the exit.

Knowing full-well the shortest distance between two points is a straight line, I decided to get a little wet. Rather than following her around the pool, I cut across it. I jumped into the shin-deep water, lifting my legs high to cross the wave pool and intercept her at the other side.

After about ten feet, I was out of breath, my brilliant mind not realizing how much harder it is to run in water. Regretful but not defeated, I picked up my pace, high-stepping like there was no tomorrow and overturning a big dude in an inner tube in the process.

"*HEY BUDDY!*" he shouted, spilling a bright red slurpee into the pool.

"Sor...UHH...eee!" I gasped, taking a deep breath and trying not to have a heart attack.

I got to the other side faster than I'd hoped, but couldn't grab the woman in black. She skidded to a stop a few feet from me, blocked by a crowd of kids. Turning, she cut through a winding nest of water slide tubes that emptied into a deeper pool somewhere to my left. Somewhere behind me, I could hear sirens approaching.

I followed her into the shadow-laden nest of plastic tubes. Above us, dark clouds were rolling in from the south, threatening the perfect summer day. With the sun slipping in and out of clouds, the already dark cluster of pipes grew darker, and the rasp of my breathing suddenly sounded very loud, as did the sound of water dripping. Sirens grew louder, but I ignored them, just as I ignored the sound of laughing children and splashing.

There was nothing. I looked at the ground, but quickly realized she wasn't wet. The only person leaving a trail was me, big wet bootprints leading back towards the wave pool.

I closed my eyes and tried something different. Usually I searched for Finch's "magical footprint," but this time I searched for a shape. In my mind's eye, I saw the knot of water slides take shape, remarkably accurate, too. Carefully, I tapped into the vael's power further, and in a moment I located myself on the little image.

Now where is she...? I wondered.

I tried harder, trying to get more from the vael. The power was limitless, yes, but it was so goddamned fickle.

When I realized the sirens weren't coming from the Ocean Hotel behind me, but instead from ahead of me, I knew I was in trouble. Unfortunately, I was just a little too late.

She'd heard the sirens, too. And realizing that she was hemmed in from the front, she turned back.

I opened my eyes just in time to see the dark shape emerge from above me, dressed in a black skin-tight body suit and wearing a black cloth mask, sinisterly hunched on a wicked S-curve of water slide piping.

"Stop!" I said, reaching for my pistol.

Unfortunately, it was back in my hotel room.

She hit me before I got my hands up in front of me. Foot-first, two thin-soled black shoes slammed into my chest, sending me spinning backwards and knocking the wind out of me. I landed on my back, with those two feet pressed flush against my chest. She leapt away, but I caught one slender ankle before she was gone. It popped from my grasp, but not before pulling her off balance. She tumbled to the ground behind me.

Wheezing, I hustled to my feet. She had caromed into a metal fixture and was slow to rise.

"Don't move, damnit!"

She rose and spun, one leg flashing out in a wicked kick. I ducked, feeling it sail over my head. I rose and struck, ramming the heel of my hand into her solar plexus.

With a gasp, she slipped backwards, slamming into a water slide. Struggling to take a breath, she fell to one knee, arms closed over her midsection.

I grabbed her bicep and pulled her upright. She let loose a pretty solid right jab to my jaw.

"Just stop!" I said, knocking her hand away. With my right foot, I pulled out her planted leg and she collapsed to the ground, breathing rapidly.

I knelt over her and pulled off the black nylon balaclava, letting loose a flood of long, red hair.

"Holy handlebar mustache!" I said in my best Gil impression. "Jane Julius, master thief. What brings

you to the beach? And why do I not think it's vacation?"

CHAPTER 13. CHANGES

I was sitting at a penthouse bar in an ocean front hotel, sipping a gin and tonic while my host got changed into "real clothes," as she put it.

How quickly things can change, eh?

After unmasking ginger Jane at the water park, we'd backtracked together to the Ocean Hotel's parking lot, slinking past a few confused parents as we avoided the police. The Rehoboth police cruiser was gone from the parking lot when we'd slipped into Jane's car–a red BMW convertible–and made our getaway.

During our awkward drive back to Rehoboth, we didn't speak much. I'd called Finch, but he didn't answer. I left a voicemail, giving an update. When that was done, I sat back and enjoyed the ride.

The storm that seemed to be threatening burned off, the scorching sun returning as we pulled into the parking lot back at Jane's Rehoboth Hotel–much nicer than ours, I have to add.

And now here I was. I sat, sipping the crisp evergreen flavor of the gin. On the small television inset behind the bar was a muted Phillies evening pre-game. The day had flown by. That's what happens when you sleep through lunch.

"What, you didn't order me anything?" a voice

said from over my shoulder.

I turned to see Jane Julius slip onto the barstool at my left. If I hadn't met her prior to today, I never would have recognized her.

Gone was the sleek black cat burglar suit; in its place was a long, royal blue high-low skirt and white sleeveless tunic. Her long red hair was pulled back, revealing her pale skin and heavily freckled face.

"Whoa," I said. "You're a woman?"

"That's funny," she said. She signaled the barman. "I'll have what he's having." She looked at me. "Gin and tonic?"

"Yep."

"A good summer drink."

"Yep."

I took a breath and cringed. Setting my glass down, I rubbed a hand across my sternum, sore from where she'd kicked me.

"Didn't hurt you too badly, did I?"

"No," I said, acting nonchalant. "I'm fine. I've got... heartburn."

She smiled as her drink was delivered. "Thank you," she said to the barman.

I watched the silent pre-game and slowly enjoyed my drink. Beside me, Jane did not speak.

After a few minutes, I said, "So are you going to come clean, or what?"

"No," she said. "Of course not."

"Why not?"

"I don't work for you, Dylan," she said. "Nor do I

work *with* you. I have nothing to come clean about."

"Oh, no?"

"No."

"What were you doing at that hotel?"

She licked her lips and set her drink down. "Looking for a room. My reservation ends here in two days."

"Downgrading, eh?"

"Just keeping my options open."

"Do you always go prospecting in your catsuit?"

"It's not a catsuit."

"Do you always go out prospecting in your weird skin suit?"

She took a sip of her drink. "Those are my work clothes," she said.

"Yes," I said. "I know that. What were you doing?"

She turned to face me for the first time, smiling coyly. "Listen, Dylan. I brought you back here because I knew that you wouldn't just let me walk away. Believe me when I say that I'm just playing along; I'm just being polite. If you think for a minute that I'm going to tell you *anything* of any value, you're being foolish."

I sighed. "We can..." I pondered what we could do. Unfortunately she was a step ahead of me.

"Do what?" she asked. "You don't work for the police. You can turn me in, but they won't have anything to charge me with except failing to pay to enter that water park. In that case, you also didn't pay. And I could just say I was running from you. You were chasing me, if you don't remember."

"Yes, I remember."

"Good. So, as I was saying, I was just being polite in bringing you here. First of all, you clearly had no ride–I did not see that abomination that your boss drives, and second, I knew that you'd want to 'grill' me for information. So if you're finished grilling me, why not polish off that drink and leave? My well of courtesy has run dry."

I exhaled. *Perhaps I can use the vael on her?* I thought. Who was I kidding? My control over the vael was worse than Gil's driving. And use it to do what? If anything, I would probably make her head explode or something, and while I didn't particularly like Jane Julius, I didn't want to kill her.

In the mirror over the bar, I watched the ocean, my eyes sometimes wandering over to Jane. In the reflection, I noticed something. I put my drink down and turned to look at her. She ignored me.

On the inside of her right arm was a scar, a scar I recognized a little too well.

"You were in Afghanistan?" I asked.

She took a drink from her gin and tonic. "Yes," she said. She looked at me and turned her arm over, revealing a seven inch scar that ran along the inside of her arm, from the center of her bicep down past her elbow a few inches down her forearm. Flanking the scar on either side were faint marks from where staples had held the wound closed.

"Shrapnel?" I asked.

She nodded. "A couple years ago. I didn't serve

for long. It was an IED."

"I've got a beauty to match that," I said. "But I think this is a shirts-on kind of establishment."

"You served?"

I nodded. "The last battle I was in was Wanat. A claymore left a nice reminder of Nuristan, a nice reminder that it's good to be home."

"Close call?"

I nodded. "A Chinook carried me and two others out. They thought I was a dead man."

"And now you do this?"

"What's that supposed to mean?"

"Now you work for Abercrombie on his crusades?"

I took a sip. "It could be a lot worse."

"It could be better."

"Oh? I could be a thief?"

"I do what I want, take the jobs that I want, go where I want."

"Yeah, well, I help people."

Now she took a sip. "I have a good reminder of what happens when I try to help people."

"You enlisted," I said. "You must have wanted to do it."

"I did," she said. "I was a fool."

"And now you do what you want?"

"Yes, I do."

"What were you doing today?"

She smiled. "Scouting–"

"–hotels, yeah, you told me."

"That's right."

"What are you doing in Rehoboth?"

"What are *you* doing in Rehoboth?" she counted.

"Vacation."

"Me too. Are you going to tell me why you were at the Ocean Hotel?" she asked.

"I'd be happy to tell you, if you tell me."

She turned to face me, smiling seductively. "It looks like... your friends are here."

"Jane!" Gil's voiced chimed out. "Jane Julius, well I'll be wrapped in bacon and fried in Kool Aid! It's been... um?"

"Twenty-nine days," Finch's voice added.

"Twenty-nine days! Not nearly long enough..."

Jane put down her drink and looked over my shoulder. "Abercrombie," she said, not warmly. "And your... associate."

"Hey, lady!"

"Hello, Ms. Julius," Finch said.

"Wanna get a table?" Gil asked. "I'm *starved*. This is your place, Jane? Nice digs. Not shaped like a castle though. Not like our place."

"I prefer four or five stars, yes. Not... castles."

"Although she's apparently looking to downgrade," I said, turning around on my stool to face Gil.

She smiled tightly. "Yes, quite."

"Do they have grub here?" Gil asked.

"Yes, of course."

The Boss turned and waved at the host. "Garçon!" he said. "A table, por favor!"

***

We were overlooking the sea. Some stories below us, the boardwalk was filling up as the sun began to sink behind the hotel, casting its orange glow across the waves. Gil and Finch ordered drinks, and as we looked over our menus, we made small talk.

Gil started:

"So Jane, what in the name of holy hell are you doing here? And don't lie, because I'll know it!"

"On vacation."

"Oh neat," he said. "So are we! Have you ever had an Old Time Photo taken? The kind where you dress up like a cowboy and–"

"Boss," I said. "She's not–"

"I knew she was lying! Nothing eludes me," he interrupted. He turned to her. "Wanna try again, lady?"

"No."

He sighed. "You're a pretty tough cookie to crack," he said. "Okay, let me ask you another thing. Why, oh why did you take that book?"

She smiled. "I'm sorry?"

"The book. You know..." he glanced around. "*Y Ddraig Goch...*"

I sighed. I had done an admirable job *not* thinking about the damned grimoire in question since the debacle at Callowleigh's *Library of Doom* a month ago, but now here it was, back again.

"Ah, *that* book."

"Ms. Julius," Finch said. "I was not present for the adventure in question, but from what I learned during the debriefing, you were quite aware of its powers. And yet you still chose to steal it."

"That's right," she said.

"Do you mind if I ask why?"

"No," she said, accepting a fresh drink from the waiter. "As long as you don't mind if I don't answer."

"Jane..." Gil growled.

She sighed. "Of course I am aware of its powers," she said, taking a sip of her second gin and tonic. "Which is exactly why I was hired to steal it."

"Money," Gil said. "You know I could have given you a *jillion* times what anyone else could offer you."

"But you didn't offer me a 'jillion' times anything," she said, using air quotes. "You wanted me to simply let you have it."

"Yeah, I did. I'll admit it. But some things are more important than money, Jane."

"I," she said slowly, "am the last person you need to remind of that."

"I'm not so sure about that," Gil said. He turned to me. "Where'd you find her?"

"At the hotel," I said. "Sneaking around."

"Sneaking around?" Gil said, twitching his mustache in thought. "Hmmm. Pretty shady, Janey."

"I don't imagine you'd like to tell us who purchased the book, would you?" Finch asked.

She laughed and took a drink, ignoring the question. "Shall we order?" she asked.

"No," Finch said, "I don't believe we should. I think we have had enough of your company, Ms. Julius."

Jane opened her mouth to respond and stopped. She looked at Gil's face, then Finch's, then mine. She frowned and put her drink down on the table.

"I see," she said. From her skirt's pocket, she pulled a few bills. "I envy your position from atop your tower of moral absolutes."

Finch shrugged. "And we've had enough of your obfuscations."

"We've got this round, Jane," Gil said, nodding at her money.

She looked up at him, her eyes steely. She peeled a twenty off the top and dropped it on the table. "Only my friends buy my drinks," she said.

With that, she was gone.

***

"That was chilly," Gil said, mocking a shiver.

"A curious woman," Finch said. "You two have spent more time with her, but I find her quite fascinating nonetheless."

"You got a girlfriend, old man!" Gil said, laughing. "Or have you forgotten about Lizzy?"

The corner of Finch's mouth twitched, his version of a smile. "No, of course not."

"Was that really necessary?" I asked.

"What?"

"Sending her away? A little rude, wouldn't you say?"

Gil shrugged. "Yeah, I guess it was. But this is a bit of a sticky wicket we're in–"

"–and she may be involved," Finch said.

That idea had not escaped me, but it still didn't seem right. "I know," I said. "I just... I don't know."

"She doesn't mind!" Gil said. "She's Jane Julius, master thief!"

"Do you really think she's involved with the kidnappings?"

"Not with that," Gil said, "no."

"But her presence at the Ocean Hotel is remarkably fortuitous," Finch said.

"I mean, yeah," I said. "But I can't imagine that she would be involved with kidnapping–"

"Hey what'd you learn at the hotel place?" Gil interrupted.

"Very little," I said. "What about you guys? And where did you go? Can you tell me now?"

Gil smiled. Beside him, Finch leaned forward. "We met with Rehoboth's City Manager, a guy named Michael Banning."

"The City what?"

"The City Manager," Finch said. "A City Manager handles a lot of administrative duties, working with the Mayor to supervise the day to day operation of most of a city's departments and staff."

"I figured you'd be meeting with the Mayor, honestly," I said.

"Apparently Mayor Kane was busy today," Gil said, rolling his eyes. "I must be losing my pull!"

"Okay, well what did you meet with the City Manager about? The dirty deputy?"

"No, no," Gil said. "We'll take that up with Sheriff Huggybear himself. We talked about the media."

"The media?"

"Yup," Gil said. He looked at his menu again. "Do you think they have chicken nuggets here?" he asked.

"No," Finch and I said.

"Why are you talking about the media?"

"Ms. Madame Clarissa," Finch said. "Do you remember what she said about a larger investigation?"

"Yeah."

"We spoke with the City Manager about why the state police were not involved, let alone the Federal Bureau of Investigations or–"

"–or why there's no stink about this in the press," Gil said, leaning forward.

"What did you find out?" I asked.

"Well," Gil said, dropping his menu, "that's the thing: we didn't!"

"What do you mean?"

"The meeting proved to be remarkably... useless," Finch said. "We outlined our concerns and the numerous reasons we were troubled."

"And?"

"And he essentially dismissed us. Even after we mentioned contacting the press."

"As a matter of fact, he gave us a card for somebody at the FBI!" Gil said.

"Yes, indeed he did," Finch said. He dug into his pocket and removed a business card. He handed it to me.

"Special Agent Jonathan Allagash," I read. "Is this guy legit?"

"We haven't called him," Gil said, "and I doubt we will."

"Why?"

"This whole thing stinks, big man!" Gil said. "If it stinks, and we know it stinks, and they know we know it stinks, why am I gonna waste time calling one of their people who is gonna tell me how it doesn't stink?"

"Uh..."

"Exactly!"

"We had another idea on the way back," Finch said.

"Oh?"

He pulled his cell phone out of his pocket. "Yes," he said. "We use a different tact."

"What is that."

"Mrs. Bascombe," Finch said.

"Willa? Why?"

"Follow the money, big man," Gil said, signaling

the waiter. "We get Willa to look into everybody's bank accounts. We find big money that doesn't belong and we know who's got their fingers in the pie." He looked at us as the waiter arrived. "Okay, you guys ready to order?" he asked.

"No," Finch and I said together.

"Okay, great! I'll have chicken nuggets!" Gil said.

"Chicken nuggets, sir?" the waiter asked.

"Yeah!"

The waiter scribbled something, frowning. He looked at Finch, who sighed.

"Chicken Caesar salad, please," Finch said.

"And you sir?" the waiter turned to me.

"Just a cheeseburger, I guess. No fries. Side salad instead, please?"

The waiter nodded.

"Thank you," we all said in unison.

Finch held the phone out to me. "Would you like to call Mrs. Bascombe?" he asked me.

I reached out to take the phone and then stopped. Willa and I definitely had a connection. I liked her... *a lot*, and I think she liked me. Trouble was that she was married, and neither of us would ever do anything considering. I liked her, but I needed to keep my distance for both of our sakes.

"No," I said. "You got this."

Finch withdrew the phone, looking vaguely confused. "All right," he said.

I ignored his look and took a sip of my drink, which *clink*ed empty. "Where's the waiter?" I asked, feeling the sudden urge for a drink.

Beside me, Finch had his phone to his ear. "Yes, Mrs. Bascombe," he said. "Yes, it's Finch... I'm doing very well, and you? ...Lovely."

"He loves this," Gil said, smiling as he shook his head. "He doesn't get computers really, and because she does he thinks it's a magical thingy, so he is always like '*oooh, oooh*, let's call Willa!' I swear, his life changed when he learned about the interweb thing. Unlike me. I don't give a flying banana about that interwebs."

"Yes, I need you to see what you can find out on a number of suspects based on their financial records... Exactly... Yes, Mayor Alicia Kane, City Manager Michael Banning, Sheriff R. Lee Huggins..." he covered the phone's mouthpiece. "Who else?" he asked softly.

"Hotel owner Fred Raleigh," I said.

"...Fred Raleigh," Finch repeated.

Gil lifted the FBI agent's business card from the table and waved it in Finch's face.

"...Special Agent Jonathan Allagash," Finch continued.

Gil looked at me. "Anybody else?" he asked.

I shook my head.

"...and check the financial records of Claire Donnegan," Finch said. "Yes, *that* Claire Donnegan... Look a little deeper... Thank you, Mrs. Bascombe... Yes, goodbye."

He ended the call and pocketed the phone. "And now," he said, "we wait."

CHAPTER 14. SHE

I liked that hotel, and I liked the view of the ocean in the setting sun, so even when I began to feel sluggish–the consequences of an all-nighter–I decided to stay and finish my drink, adjourning back to the bar to watch the Phillies game as Gil and Finch made their exit.

It was quite a moment of déjà vu when Jane reappeared in the seat to my left, much as she had two hours earlier. The only difference now was that the bar was nearly empty, and outside the sky was in its rich twilight mode.

"You're still in my bar," she said, ordering another gin and tonic.

"Sorry about that," I said, taking a sip of my drink–a Manhattan; I'd switched. "Want me to hit the trail?"

"No," she said. "I, unlike some others, am not so specific about my drinking company."

"Yes, you are," I said.

"All right, I can be a little choosy, I admit."

I turned to her. "I'm sorry about earlier. I... I was a little mad at you, too. But I wouldn't have asked you to leave."

She shrugged, swirling ice around her glass. "I

shouldn't have been offended. I should be used to it by now," she said. "Things are always more complicated than they seem."

I finished my drink and contemplated leaving. The ice in the empty glass rattled, and I stared at it.

Jane looked up. "Are you going to order another round?"

"I shouldn't," I said. "I've had a few of these over the past two hours."

"So have I," she said, taking another sip of her drink.

"You've been gone for over an hour."

She smiled. "The rooms here are nice. The mini-bars are fully stocked."

"They say drinking alone is a warning sign of alcoholism and depression. They say it's unhealthy."

"Drinking alone is not unhealthy," she said, "only unsociable."

"Why did you sell the book, Jane?"

"Because that's what I was hired to do. And I was paid a great deal of money to do it."

"You knew it was wrong."

"It was very complicated"

"And why are you here?"

She caught the bartender's eye. "I believe the gentleman will have another," she said.

I dug in my pocket for my wallet. "And one more for the lady," I said.

"What did I say at dinner?" Jane said, turning a sharp eye in my direction.

"What?"

"I said only my friends buy my drinks."

"Then you should not object," I said, handing the bartender a pair of bills in exchange for the two drinks.

"Thank you."

I watched the silent Phillies game on the bar's TV. They were playing the Rockies. I sighed as our reliever gave up a soaring home run over the right field fence.

"Are you from Philadelphia?" she asked.

"Yes. Are you?"

"No."

"Do you live in Philadelphia?"

She glanced at me, a hint of paranoia on her face. Finally, she said, "Sometimes."

"Where are you from?"

"Here and there."

"I could find you, you know. I know you served in Afghanistan; I know your name."

"That's not my real name," she said.

"Of course it's not," I said. "Is anything about you genuine?"

"I resent that," she said.

"Sorry."

"Are you here because of the kidnappings?"

I looked at her. She was staring straight ahead. "Yes," I said. "What do you know about them?"

"Very little," she said. "But I can tell you something true, something genuine."

"What is that?"

She turned to me. "I have nothing to do with those kidnappings. I would never do that."

"I believe you," I said. And I did. Unquestionably. There was a fierce honesty in her eyes that I could not question, an understated but immovable sense of what was right and wrong. Without a doubt, I knew what she'd told me was true.

She did not respond, only attended to her drink.

I turned back and watched the Phillies change pitchers. Another loss was imminent. Behind us the sun had slipped below the horizon, and darkness had fallen. Somewhere to my right I heard a jazz pianist play the opening notes to "Body and Soul," and I could all but hear Billie Holiday's voice accompanying it.

"You want to get out of here?" Jane said, turning to me.

I looked at her and raised my eyebrows. "Really?"

"Yes."

"Yeah," I said. "I'd like that."

CHAPTER 15. LADY DAZE

I woke up alone in a strange room–that sounds like the beginning of a horror story.

This was not a horror story. As a matter of fact, I felt really good.

"Jane?" I asked, slipping into my jeans. "Jane?"

I checked the bathroom. Definitely empty. No note, no regrets. Sometime in the early morning hours she'd packed and left. I got dressed and made the bed before leaving myself.

On the way down in the elevator, I checked my phone and found a text message from a number I didn't recognize. It read, "*I had fun last night.*" That was it.

Texting wasn't my thing, so I laboriously hammered out, "*Me too*" and hit send before saving the number.

In the lobby, I walked quickly past the concierge and stepped out into the sunlight. It was a little after eight, and it was already hot out. Despite the intense heat and humidity, I felt great. After our tryst last night, I'd had the best sleep in I didn't know how long. It was really nice sleeping next to someone again.

Walking through the boardwalk's growing throng

of people, I reminded myself not to over-romanticize what happened. I'm not the sort of person who does that, but it had been so long I was afraid I might, and one night with Jane was enough to know *she* certainly wouldn't romanticize anything. I liked her—a lot, as a matter of fact—but I didn't think I could ever apply the word "love" to a relationship with her, and that was okay. I know it was only one night, but sometimes you get a feel for these things immediately.

I took a right on Rehoboth Avenue, turning my back on the ocean, and walked inland towards our hotel. At the drug store I took a newspaper off the rack and dropped cash on the counter. Opening the newspaper, I half expected to see some story about the previous day's escapades. Something about the City Manager getting bullied by a couple of weirdos from Philadelphia; or how a pair of vagrants entered a Lewes water park called Kokomo Joe's without paying admission. There was even an unsettling fear in the back of my mind that I would find a story about another kidnapping. If that had happened, there is literally no way I would have escaped that guilt after the night I'd had.

Thankfully, the front page held nothing but a story about beach erosion and the Phillies loss I'd witnessed.

I was still reading about the Phillies game when I walked into my hotel lobby and took the elevator up. I was still reading when I turned the corner and stopped. There was someone knocking on my door. I lowered the paper.

It was Willa.

I tried to act cool. "Uhhhh," I said.

She turned, tightening the messenger bag on her shoulder. "Where have you been?" she asked. "I've been out here knocking for twenty minutes. I was about to get the concierge to unlock it because I assumed you were dead."

I closed the paper in a decidedly uncool crumpling of paper. "What are you doing here?" I asked.

"Finch called me last night, remember?" She stepped back to allow me to unlock the door. "I figured I'd save myself the long phone calls and just come down–" she stopped. "You have something on your neck..." she trailed off as I opened the door.

"What is it?" I asked.

I dropped the newspaper on my dresser and looked in the mirror.

It was lipstick. Well, shit.

"It's nothing," I said. "Um, suntan lotion, that's all."

"Crimson suntan lotion? Do you really think I don't know what that is?"

I turned around to look at her and bit my lip. "No," I said. "But–"

"Anyway," she said, turning away and taking a seat in a nearby chair. "It's just easier for me to come down. I was up late last night–*working*, digging up this information for you guys on these names."

I grabbed some clean clothes out of my suitcase and flipped on the bathroom light. "What did you find?" I asked, closing the door.

"Weird stuff," she said. Through the bathroom door, her voice was muffled, so I told her to hold on.

The lipstick streak on my neck was... hard to ignore. It was a slash of crimson on a patch of pretty pale skin. I wet a washcloth and wiped it away.

I washed up a bit, brushed my teeth, and got dressed. A shower would have been a great idea, but I didn't have time. I dried my face and opened the door.

"Did you hear what I said?" she asked.

"No," I said, sitting down on the bed to pull on clean socks.

"I said we were supposed to meet Gil and Finch downstairs twenty minutes ago."

"I'll be ready in a second."

"This place is a mess," she said, looking around.

"I wasn't expecting any guests," I said.

"Good thing you didn't bring your date back here."

"It wasn't a date," I said. "And are we going to have a problem with this?"

"I'm just saying," she said, smiling. "Your room is a mess."

I tied my shoes and stood. "Let's go."

The elevator ride down was quiet. Willa fidgeted in her bag, pulling out files of paperwork one by one before slipping them back in. I checked my phone so I would have something to do.

In the lobby, she lead the way towards the room where continental breakfast was usually served. It was uncharacteristically quiet.

Gil and Finch had taken over a big round table in the corner, large enough for at least six. Gil had food spread around him like debris. Donuts, danish, muffins, grapes, juice, and about four of the single-serve boxes of *Count Chocula* cereal. He sat chowing down on cereal, scratching at his sunburned face. Across from him, Finch was sipping tea and eating an English muffin.

"Look who decided to get out of bed!" Gil said, looking up. "Glad you could join the world of the living."

"Yeah, yeah. Sorry I slept in for a change."

"You're usually up at like 5:30, man. I was gettin' worried."

"Sorry." When Gil says he is worried, he isn't kidding. It is one of his more endearing qualities.

"It's okay," he said. "So you found the bum, eh, Willa?" Gil asked, smiling. When she didn't respond, he continued, turning to me. "What were you doin'? Workin' out? Buyin' some taffy? Joggin'? I was there lookin' for you like, *really* early. I left those double-stuffed Oreos in there and I had a craving, man. I couldn't figure out what you'd be doin' so early in the—"

"Boss," Finch interrupted. When Gil turned to him, Finch simply shook his head. "Why don't we get started?"

"Oh, well let 'em eat why dontcha?" He turned to us. "You guys want some coffee? Or chocolate milk?"

"I'll have some coffee," she said, taking a seat. "Thanks, Gil."

"My pleasure! And get somethin' to eat, please! You're wasting away!"

"I ate already," she said. "I got something in the car."

"I'm gonna grab a plate," I said, taking my leave. I got some cereal, an orange, a cheese danish, and a cup of coffee.

When I sat back down, Willa had spread a layer of papers over most of the table.

"All right," I said. "What have we got?"

"This is..." she sighed. "Sorry," she said. "I have all these documents," she gestured at the jungle of paperwork, "but it's... well, what I found was no good."

"What do you mean?" Finch asked, lowering his tea cup.

"These are bank records, credit reports, credit card statements, mortgage paperwork, and about a dozen other things, all for the people you asked me to look into."

"Wow, you got this just last night?" I asked.

"Yeah," she said. "That was easy. Finding the data is easy for me. The real work is actually interpreting this data."

"Okay," I said. "What did you find when you did that?"

"That's the problem," she said, pushing away a stack of documents, annoyed. "I found, nothing and something."

Gil raised his hand. "I don't get it."

"It's like..." she sighed again. "I've been trying to

think of a way to explain this since last night. The only analogy I can make is to an image in a magazine. Sometimes you look at an image in a magazine and you know it's been touched up. Something about it has been edited or changed or airbrushed; something about what you're seeing isn't quite right. Little things here and there begin to add up. Your eye isn't picking out egregious errors of anatomy, but you can tell that something has been fiddled with. Do you know what I mean?"

"Are you saying that about these?" Gil said, waving his hand over the piles of paper.

"Yes," she said. "Absolutely. Something about this stuff just isn't right."

"Can you give me an example?" I asked.

"Like..." she flipped a few pages. "Here. City Manager Michael Banning's bank account is clean. He makes 68K a year, he pays his bills on time, and he likes buying silk ties online. Problem is that he's got missing deposits. His bank account is showing activity; money is going *out*. The trouble is that more is going out than going in. It's like the transaction log has been edited." She flipped a few more pages. "Here's another. Special Agent Jonathan Allagash has just paid a downpayment on a house on the bay outside of Annapolis. The downpayment was three hundred thousand. He makes 90K a year. But it didn't raise any red flags, it didn't warrant any questions. It's like the fact that he did it was erased."

"A three hundred thousand dollar *deposit*?" I asked. "It must be a mansion!"

Willa flipped a few pages before pulling one

loose. She handed it to me. "It is, look."

I took the paper and nodded. "Yep, it is."

"These financial records aren't right. Things have been doctored and covered up. Dangerous questions have been shelved, incriminating evidence has disappeared."

"Who looks funny?" Gil said. "Does the Sheriff? Sheriff Huggybear?"

"Sheriff Huggins looks clean," Willa said.

"What about Claire Donnegan?" Finch asked.

"Madame Clarissa is also clean," Willa said.

"What about the hotel guy?" I asked. "Fred Raleigh?"

She shook her head again. "Nope. But the May-or doesn't look great."

I sighed. "Well, that sucks," I said.

"But you did not find anything directly incriminating," Finch said.

"No, I didn't."

"All righty," Gil said. "Now what?"

"I've got a meeting tomorrow with a guy I know who lives in Dover. He's a forensic accountant. He's going to take a closer look at some of these things for me."

"Hopefully your friend can Magic Eye some of that stuff," Gil said.

"Eye..." I put down my coffee, my brain keying in on that word, jogging a memory. "Ugh, damn, I completely forgot." I dug my phone out of my pocket and opened up the pictures. There waiting for me was the photo I'd taken of the chalk eye at the Ocean Hotel. "What do you make of this, Finch?" I asked, sliding the phone across the table to him.

"Where did you take this?" he asked.

"At the hotel. I forgot about it until just now."

Finch squinted at the small screen. "It's definitely one of the witch runes," he said.

Willa's eyebrows rose. "Sorry, but did you say 'witch runes'?"

"Yeah," Gil said. "It's a whole... *witchy* thing."

"The eye rune is complicated," Finch said, taking a sip of tea, "but from what I remember, it means that how we see things will be changing. It also means that strong magical forces are at play. Things could potentially be turned upside down, and our expectations could be dashed."

"Great," I said. "I was hoping I was wrong; I was hoping it was just some jackass kid's doodle."

"Unfortunately, it isn't," he said, passing my phone back to me.

"Okay, well... what's next?" I asked, pocketing my phone.

"Here's the scoop, kids," Gil said, wiping his mouth with a napkin. "Our reservations at this fine establishment are coming to an end. Because of the ongoing nature of our investigation, however, I have been forced to acquire new lodgings for us."

"What's wrong with this place?" I asked.

"They have no available openings," Gil said. "So I was forced to buy a condo in the Henlopen."

"You did what?"

"Hey, I'm rich. Plus, I've always wanted to have a penthouse at the beach, especially after I saw that bar last night with Jane. That was pretty fly, boy. So anyway, pack your bags, because today we check out and move into our new place up on the boardwalk."

"Is there room for–"

"It has five bedrooms, kiddo," Gil said, smiling. "You are most certainly welcome."

"Great."

"So back down here ASAP and we'll make our way over. Unfortunately, team, this is just getting more complicated."

We adjourned, taking the elevator upstairs together and going to our separate rooms. Willa stuck with me, resuming her seat while I scraped clothes into my suitcase and crammed it closed.

"So... Jane? Is that the thief you guys told me about? From the asylum place?"

"Yeah," I said, immediately regretting telling her that story.

"It was her?"

"What?"

"She was the one? Really? A thief?"

"She's not as bad as she sounds," I said, zipping my suitcase shut.

"International thief of mystery who screwed you guys out of a priceless grimoire that could unleash the Devil?"

"That's her."

"She sounds pretty bad."

I lifted the suitcase. "We're not getting married or anything," I said with a sigh.

Willa looked at me and smiled. "Well, if you're having fun–"

"I am, she's a lot of fun," I said, realizing how much that must have hurt for her to say. "Now let's go."

***

In the lobby, Willa helped Gil carry a second suitcase that was apparently filled with Legos. As we walked out the door, a young bellboy called me back to the desk.

"I'll catch up," I told the gang as I turned back.

At the desk, a chubby man with glasses smiled at me. "You have a phone call, sir."

"Me?"

"Yes." He gestured to a phone on a small table in a nook against the wall. I put down my suitcase and walked over to the nook.

"Hello?"

"I imagine you'd all but forgotten about us, Mr. Dylan."

"Who is this?"

"Is that any way to speak to your overseer?"

"Greely," I said. Just saying his name made my stomach turn to ice. Arthur Greely was my vampire handler representing the vamp's governing body, the Battery. I'd made a deal to save Willa's life in my inaugural Zeros adventure, trading my services for their assistance. The contract had served me well in keeping her alive, but I'd always known I couldn't avoid the remaining obligations forever.

"Is this a bad time?"

"Why are you calling me on the house phone?"

"I don't know how secure your private line is. Does your employer pay for it? Does he check your records?"

"No, he doesn't do either. We actually trust each other."

Greely laughed. It sounded like a cat hissing. "So he knows about this arrangement?"

Guilt stabbed me like a knife. "Well, no–"

"Then since you are so open and honest, I apologize for inconveniencing you as such," he said, sounding about as disingenuous as humanly possible. "I will call you on your private line next time."

"*What do you want, Greely?*" I asked, not kindly. "I am becoming conspicuous."

"It's time to fulfill your first contractual obligation," he said, sounding terribly pleased. "We need you to come in."

"I can't, not now–"

"Now, Mr. Dylan. I expect you in Philadelphia by noon. No questions, no pardons. There's a job we need done, and you're the man to do it."

"But that's–"

The line went dead.

I hung up the phone and cursed under my breath.

"Problem, big guy?"

I turned around to see Gil standing in the doorway, looking concerned.

"Nope," I said, smiling. "Everything is perfectly fine."

What a steaming pile of BS that was.

CHAPTER 16. DO YOU HEAR ME NOW?

I drove the Tank the three blocks or so north to the Henlopen and parked in their underground garage. Together, we trudged inside with our collection of bags.

"You're pretty quiet, big man," Gil asked as we waited for any elevator.

"I'm fine," I lied, forcing a smile that I'm sure looked incredibly unnatural. Willa gave me a look and I showed her the fake smile too.

Even if I hadn't just gotten a call from the Battery, the Jane/Willa thing was already adding a bunch of stress on top of the awful kidnapping business. Hearing from Greely *really* wasn't helping matters.

"Okay," Gil said dubiously. The doors *ding*ed open and we four shuffled inside.

On the top floor, the elevator opened to a short foyer leading directly to a door. Gil pulled a ring of keys from his pocket and opened the door.

If I wasn't so distracted, I would have been impressed.

"It's fully furnished!" Willa said, dropping Gil's bags.

"Of course, I ain't sleepin' on the floor," he laughed. "It's amazing what someone will do if you add a couple of bucks to your offer. And if you tell a scary story about ghosts. Some people will believe anything about ghosts."

"You lied to these people about ghosts?" Willa asked.

"Well, I really wanted them to leave their stuff. I mean... I *paid* them and all," Gil said, smiling.

The penthouse covered most of the top floor, and it was beautifully furnished. Ringing the entire apartment was a balcony that overlooked the ocean, the boardwalk, and even the pond behind the Henlopen.

"You said there are five bedrooms?" Finch asked.

"You got it, bud."

"I believe I will unpack," Finch said, lifting his small suitcase and making his way towards the cluster of bedrooms.

Willa made her way directly towards the balcony, opening the sliding glass door and stepping outside. A rush of salty sea air flooded inside, and I took a deep breath, closing my eyes. It seemed a zen-like thing to do, and I'd hoped it would help calm me. It didn't, but it gave me an idea.

Gil was in the kitchen, opening drawers and looking around. "Perfect," he said, "everything is here, just like I asked 'em!" He opened the fridge and pulled out a can of *Mello Yello* soda. "There's even string cheese in here. Nice! And hot dogs." He opened the pantry and dug around. "I don't see any cookies, though. That is a serious problem." He turned around.

"Finch! I need help here! There aren't any cookies! Is that in-case-of-emergency box still in the Tank's trunk?"

"I'm gonna get a room," I said. "You know... unpack."

"Okie dokie," Gil said, opening his can and plopping down in front of the TV.

I walked quickly down the hall and threw my suitcase in the first room I saw that was empty. Instead of unpacking, I kept walking. Finch was in the room at the end.

"Hey, you got a minute?"

He was kneeling in front of the dresser, carefully stacking folded black pants in an open drawer. "Yes," he said. "What's wrong?"

I glanced back down the hall and closed the door.

"No," he said. "Leave it open. Closing it is suspicious."

"Privacy is a good thing," I said, a bit harried.

"It also prevents us from knowing if someone is coming." He dragged his polished shoe across the carpet. "Wall to wall is not good for hearing footsteps."

"Oh okay," I opened the door halfway.

"This is about the Battery, no?"

I nodded. "Greely just called me."

"On the house phone back at the Hotel?" Finch nodded. "They are incredibly suspicious. They won't call your mobile until you give them the okay."

"He wants me to come in."

"Now?"

"Yes."

"What did he say?" Finch said, taking a step closer and lowering his voice.

"He said to come in, *right now*."

"No, his actual words."

I thought for a moment. "Something like, 'it's time to fulfill your first obligation'... and 'we need you to come in.'"

"Is that all?"

"He also said, 'there's a job we need–"

"–done, and you're the man to do it?"

"Yes, exactly!"

Finch glanced down the hall and turned the TV on, selecting CNN and turning the volume up. "It's a power play," he said. "You need to call him back and tell him no."

"What do you mean–"

From down the hall, I could hear Gil chattering with Willa. His voice was getting louder.

"Your first job will set the standards for your relationship with your handler. Greely is a worm, he is trying to muscle you. If this job was as important as he's making it out to be, he'd say, 'We need your unique talent,' or something like that."

"How do you know that?"

"You forget that the Battery is a corporation; the handlers are trained," Finch said. "They have words to say and words not to say. Their training is taken very seriously, and when a handler is new they tend to lean heavily on their training. He's using the exact phrases they're trained to use. He's new and he's playing for power."

"How did you get used to this?"

Finch smiled sadly. "I've unfortunately been doing this for quite some time. And I've gone through a great number of handlers."

"So I just tell him 'no'?"

"Yes. You dictate the terms of your contract, Dylan," Finch said, lowering his voice further. "You forget that they *need* you. They did a great deal to get you on contract, and *they* need *you*."

In the hall, Gil was very close. We stepped away from the door.

"Trust me," Finch said. "Call him and tell him. You set the ground rules, you are in charge. Greely only *wishes* to be in charge."

"Do you have his number?"

Finch nodded. "I'll get it for you," he said.

At that moment, Gil walked into the room. "What are you girls doin' in here?" he asked. "Chattin' about cute boys? Pickin' out matching out-fits?"

I looked up, searching for a halfway decent excuse. Finch calmly said, "Dylan is curious about runes. He is troubled by what he found at the Ocean Hotel."

Gil nodded. "I am too, honestly. Unpack and we'll have a sit down at the table. Drink some *Mello Yello*, eat some *Fritos*, watch *Big Trouble in Little China*, and talk about what we've got goin' on. From where I stand, we've got a lot of work ahead of us."

"I agree," Finch said. He turned to me. "Why don't you get unpacked?"

***

I was in my room, uneasily unpacking when I got a text message from Finch. It was a phone number.

When Greely answered, the sound of his voice did that thing to my stomach again.

"It's me," I said.

"Yes, Mr. Dylan?"

"I'm not gonna come in today," I said.

"...I'm sorry?"

"I said I'm not gonna come in today. What I'm doing here is more important."

"What*ever* you are doing, it is certainly not more important than–"

"No," I interrupted. "You're not listening. My voice did not rise at the end of that sentence: *I am not going to come in today*. It was a statement, not a question. I'm going to stay here, finish my work, and then finish my vacation. When I'm back in Philadelphia, I will reach out to you."

"I don't know what you–"

"I'm not finished," I said. "In the future, if you need me, you text me. I will not be receiving unexpected phone calls from you. That is unacceptable. If you need me, you text me and I will reach out to you. Otherwise, I don't expect to hear from you. Do you hear me?"

There was silence on the line for a long moment, long enough to make me think he'd disconnected. He hadn't. "Yes," he said finally. "I hear you."

"Good."

"But understand, I am your very first point contact. You may be able to ignore me, but you can't ignore the Battery. The next message you receive won't be from me, Mr. Dylan, it will be from Carrion."

I bit down on my lip. "Then I look forward to his call."

With that, I hung up.

CHAPTER 17. LIFE IS A MERRY-GO-ROUND

I waited for that phone call, and a funny thing happened: the better part of a week passed.

We each had things to do, ways of passing time. Finch continued relentless research, usually spending time alone with books he'd had express shipped down from Philadelphia—or from such faraway places as San Francisco and Minneapolis. He even received a wooden crate one day stamped *GLASGOW*. At times he called Clarissa, sometimes even venturing out, books in hand, to hash out ideas and double-check his findings. As the days passed, his demeanor seemed to grow grimmer.

Gil spent most of his time watching surveillance footage that Willa had illicitly downloaded from a number of private CCTV sources. He quickly became a mainstay on the sofa, watching endless hours of blurry black and white footage of vacationers having a good time. Never did he see one of the missing children; never did he see the ominous black-shape we'd seen that night at Fort Miles.

Willa had perhaps the most maddening task of all. She spent countless hours sifting through financial records, struggling to grasp even the barest thread of evidence that could concretely be tied to any one suspect. She took two bedrooms, one to sleep in and one to organize her paperwork. On the few occasions I entered the paperwork room, I was struck by the sheer magnitude of what she was undertaking. Piles covered most of the floor. On the walls, papers she'd deemed "vitally important" were thumbtacked, each spotted with streaks of highlighter. On at least three different days, she drove up to Dover to visit her forensic accountant, always returning empty-handed.

I spent my days feeling rather ineffectual. I lacked skills in accounting and hacking, and I could not focus on research for more than a few minutes at a time. Once or twice I tried watching surveillance footage with Gil, but each time I succeeded only in falling asleep. And so I took to walking the streets, especially at night. It seems as though my time spent walking the beat as a cop was not wasted. After only two nights I had a full routine that circled Rehoboth Avenue, travelled the length of the boardwalk, and made loops throughout the back residential streets. The shopkeepers and retailers got to know me, and I got to know them. I started carrying my gun again. The presence of the .38 in my belt did not allow me to forget the duties, or what could happen if I got lax. The names Benjamin Mason Jr. and Megan Wilson were always in my head.

I thought about Jane more than I'd like to admit. The coincidence that she'd been at the Ocean Hotel was a lot to ignore. I often wondered if I'd made a terrible mistake. Was Jane behind what was happening? How clouded was my judgment? Did my actions jeopardize what we were doing? Was I now compromised? In my more grounded moments, I dismissed these fears. Late at night, when I was alone, they seemed to prey on me.

And all along, I waited for the call from Carrion, feeling that at any moment, my life could be carried away in an awful sea of change.

Days passed, and the call never came.

***

On the morning of July 2nd, Gil woke us all with exuberant shouting and banging, running up and down the hallway like a kid on Christmas morning.

"Up, up, up!" he said repeatedly. "Today is a new day!"

Almost as one, three bedroom doors opened lazily, and Willa, Finch, and I stepped out into the hall.

"What time is it?" Willa asked.

"This is wholly unnecessary," Finch said.

Having gone to sleep only about four hours earlier, I just frowned. A lot.

"I made breakfast," Gil said, smiling proudly. "It's in the dining room. Today, we pull ourselves up by our shoelaces, eat a real meal together, and assess where we are."

Finch scowled. "Is it–"

"Eggs and sausage and grits and toast and danishes and scrapple and fruit and cereal and juice and bacon and muffins and coffee and croissants and donuts and pretty much everything else!"

We three just looked at him.

"All right, so I ordered in," he said. "But it looks delicious! I set the table, at least."

Together, we walked out of the hallway, hair disheveled and wearing our pajamas. Clarissa was pouring coffee when we got to the dining room, wearing a different floral muumuu and bright smile.

"You set the table, huh?" I asked Gil.

"I helped!" he said defensively.

"Good morning all!" Clarissa said, smiling.

"Ugh, I'm sorry," Willa said. "Let me get dressed–"

"Not necessary, dear," Clarissa said, pulling a chair out. "Please, have a seat. All of you! Sit, sit!"

Perhaps too tired to object, we all sat.

"You guys were up late," Gil said. "And you look it."

We nodded. It seems I wasn't the only one plagued by our failure to accomplish anything.

"Well, you've been working hard," he continued, "and today we're gonna take stock of where we are and what comes next."

Willa, Finch, and I were quiet, belying our successes (see: failures). Gil looked at our faces, his smile never wavering. He took a seat. "Eat up!" he said. "We'll need our energy."

Finch poured himself some tea and took a croissant. Willa ladled a spoon of eggs beside a few slices of cantaloupe. I got some cereal and a cup of coffee. Clarissa buttered herself two pieces of toast and poured a tall glass of orange juice. Gil ate donuts with a glass of milk.

"All right," he said. "Who wants to go first?"

Willa put her fork down and sighed. "I've got nothing," she said miserably. "I've gone over every penny that Allagash and Banning and Kane have spent in the last four months. Nothing is adding up, but even my forensic accountant can't figure out why. Things have been doctored, but the oversight committees have either approved of their actions or simply turned their backs. Nothing is making sense, and at this point, every check and balance has gone in favor of these people."

"What's your next step?" Gil asked.

"I... I don't know. My plan was to follow the money, but as far as I'm concerned, there *is* no money. It's like there are footprints, but nothing to leave them."

"Your logic is sound," Finch said. "And perhaps the most interesting aspect is that your work has not left you empty-handed."

"What do you mean?"

"You've compiled a list of suspects."

"I haven't–"

"No, he's right," I said. "You told us that Sheriff Huggins was clean, right?"

She nodded.

"And Raleigh, the guy who owns the hotel."

"Yeah."

"Who isn't?" I asked, glancing at Clarissa, feeling a pang of guilt that we'd been suspicious of her and her motives, too.

"It looks like the two dirtiest are probably the City Manager and the FBI Agent, this guy Allagash."

"Then that's narrowed it somewhat, hasn't it?"

She nodded grudgingly. "I guess. But I haven't found anything concrete."

"What you've got is enough for now," Gil said. "If all you can do is find people who are probably dirty, it is going to keep our asses out of the fire."

"So what should I do?"

"Expand," Gil said. "Broaden your search. Pick names of those who have gotten involved in this in one way or another and look into them. You know, like secondary characters!"

"Expand..." Willa said slowly.

"Yeah, if nothing else, it'll tell us who we can trust."

She nodded. "Fair enough. I can do that."

Gil smiled. "Who's next?" he asked.

"I'll go, because I've got very little to say," I said, clearing my throat. "I've taken to patrolling at night. My experience tells me that the boardwalk after dark is a prime location for the next kidnapping, so I've got a route that I vary depending on the night. I've interviewed nearly two-dozen clerks and managers at just as many shops or restaurants, looking for information regarding any of the missing children or the figure in black. I've learned nothing else, except that the streets off Rehoboth Avenue are too dark for a police patrol to accomplish much. The streetlights are too dim and unevenly spaced, and there are a huge number of unattended children for a town that has recently had two kidnappings."

"All right, what's *your* next step?"

I shook my head. "I'm not sure," I admitted. "I can't tell if one non-uniformed person walking the beat accomplishes anything in a town with this many streets and alleyways. I feel like I'm doing something good when I'm out there, but if it's actually worth anything, I can't tell."

"You need to talk to the Sheriff," Finch said. "We've pussyfooted around the PD for too long as it is. We either need to point them in the right direction or get them to accept our assistance."

"But you saw how it went last time–"

"We can't give up," Gil said. "I don't think we can win without their help."

Willa nodded. Finch and Clarissa looked impassive.

"But we need something to give them," I said. "Hard evidence. We've got nothing right now, nothing to buy their loyalty or even point them in the right direction. We're empty-handed!"

"Not quite," Finch said. "I believe I've found something."

"What?"

"First, I must apologize for missing this, it is remarkably simple, so simple that it never occurred to me. Ms. Donnegan was the first to notice my oversight, which is why I am quite glad she is here with us today."

Clarissa nodded bashfully. "It was nothing," she said. "I got lucky."

"You were perceptive," Finch said. "That is no small feat, especially when you've no idea what to look for." He looked at us. "Today is July 2nd, we are in what is called the waning crescent of the moon. Megan Wilson was taken twelve days ago, on June 21st. Exactly two weeks prior to that, on June 7th, Benjamin Mason Jr. was taken. Ms. Wilson was kidnapped on a new moon. Mr. Mason was kidnapped on the last full moon."

"So you're saying that they're following a pattern?" Willa asked.

"It's more than that," Clarissa said.

"They are following the phases of the moon," Finch said.

"Wiccans rely heavily in the phases of the moon, believing it plays a key role on the energies that surround us," Clarissa continued. "If a Wiccan is involved in the kidnappings, it would make sense that they followed the phases of the moon."

"All right," I said, "so I guess it's definitely witches. Using that info, can we predict when the next kidnapping will take place?"

"In two days," Willa said. "You said Megan Wilson was kidnapped twelve days ago, right? Then it's two days away." She looked at me, her face ashen.

"That's the Fourth of July," I said. "It's a logistical nightmare, even if we had a full police force at our disposal–"

"Which we don't," Gil said. "So that means we need to get our nose down to the grindstone. We need evidence," he said. "And help."

"I'll broaden my search," Willa said. "If we can get additional suspects, maybe then we'll be able to get them under surveillance. What if we spook them and they miss the full moon?"

"As far as I can tell," Finch said, "it won't matter. In two weeks, there will be a new moon, offering another opportunity to take a child."

"Why are they doing it?" I asked. "How many children do they need? Are the children even alive?"

Those were three bad questions, but it was about time someone asked them.

"I don't know," Finch said, softly. "I have been going through all my books, and I have not found anything, nothing that points in the correct direction at all. No indicators, no patterns, no history."

"So there may be no end in sight," I said softly.

"I don't know," he said. "But it is possible."

"What about you, Clarissa?" Gil asked. "Have you been working on what I asked?"

She nodded, her head hanging low. "I've been searching for the coven," she said. "I feel like I've canvassed the entire town, but it's as if they up and disappeared."

"Can we take that as some indication of guilt?" I asked.

No one had an answer. If they were missing, it's not like it mattered. We couldn't find them anyway.

"Well, now what?" Willa finally asked.

"We've got two days," Gil said. "If we haven't made any headway by then, another kid is going to get taken." He looked at each of us, his face uncharacteristically grim. "So finish your eggs and toast and whatever, my friends; we've got work to do."

CHAPTER 18. WHIRLWIND

If urgency had not been playing a crucial role before, it certainly took center stage once Finch laid out the timetable for us. What had once been a pressing–albeit temporally vague–threat had become dire. Another child was about to disappear.

So at 10 o'clock in the morning on July 3rd, I showed up at the Sheriff's department, dressed in a white button down, grey jacket, and jeans for my appointment with Sheriff R. Lee Huggins himself. It was no small feat getting the appointment, and I was lucky to get it before the 4th. In a manilla folder under one arm I held a few documents, certain incriminating papers Willa had obtained in regards to Huggins' deputy Michael Donnelly aka William Leachman, wanted for questioning in the murder of his wife. Not exactly a fugitive, but damning evidence nonetheless.

I walked inside, a light layer of sweat on my forehead. A chubby woman sat behind a broad wooden desk, a pen behind her right ear.

"Can I help you?" she asked.

"I've an appointment with Sheriff Huggins at 10," I said.

"One moment, please." She lifted the handset and spoke softly into the receiver. After a moment, she hung up and said, "He'll see you now. This way."

She stood and lead me through a door. Beyond lay a long corridor that looked familiar. Against the right wall was a long wooden bench, the same bench Gil and I had warmed on our first visit to the small station.

The secretary opened the door and showed me inside, closing it behind me. Sheriff Huggins sat at his desk, frowning. Unfortunately, he remembered me.

"What... what can I do for you?" he asked, probably rephrasing a much ruder question he would have preferred to ask.

"I know we didn't get started off on the best foot," I said, "but I want to try it again."

"Why?"

"Why did we get started off on the wrong foot?"

"No," he said, leaning forward. "I remember that. I remember that you started a fight on my beach."

"I didn't *start* a fight—"

"And since then, you've taken up some kind of night patrol, walking my streets looking for who knows what. What the hell do you expect to find?"

I'll admit, I was surprised Huggins knew I had taken up my little patrol. In a resort town, it was easy for cops to soft-pedal things and relax. If Huggins was soft-pedaling anything, he wasn't showing it. Regardless, he was getting angrier by the minute, and I needed to get in front of this thing before it got out of control.

"Who said I'm looking—"

"Also, if I frisked you right now, what would I

find?"

Thankfully–because I'm not a complete idiot, I'd left my pistol back in the Henlopen before I'd come to the station.

"You'd find *nothing*, as a matter of–"

"All right, what if I picked you up at 2AM on the corner of 1st and Olive? Would you be clean then?"

"Anything I carry I'm licensed to carry, okay? You think I'm some jackass perp, but I'm not."

"How do I know that?" he asked angrily, making no pretense of lowering his voice. "I don't know you from Adam, buddy!"

"Check my police service record, or my military record, or the three years I spent working private security–"

"Private security is a joke–"

"No shit, but working as a Philadelphia city cop for two years isn't anything to shake a stick at. And between that and Afghanistan and Baghdad, I think I've done enough to prove that I'm on the level. More than writing parking tickets and citing chickenshit kids for littering. So why not get down off your high horse for a second and listen to what I came here to say?"

Huggins' face was red. He stared at me like he'd like to go 9 rounds. I felt much the same. It's funny how quickly I can go from 0 to Hulk Smash.

"All right," Huggins said, taking a deep breath. "Talk."

"You're in over your head, Sheriff. Even if you know what you're doing, and it sounds like you do, you're still in over your head. Philly cops don't even handle kidnappings alone, let alone multiple kidnappings. This is what the Feds do–"

"We called the Feds–"

"Yeah, a Special Agent Allagash," I said. "I know. That guy is one of two things: stupid or crooked. After the third time you got blown off, you should've tried somebody else. And where the hell are the State Cops? You shouldn't be handling this alone!"

"You think you need to tell me that?" he asked angrily, his voice rising further. "I've been screaming to high hell for help, and I've gotten nothing, absolutely jackshit nothing. And now you come in here–"

"Come in here to *help* you. Ask around about me. Call the Philly PD. Captain Martin McGraw. He'll give you references out the ass, but don't act like I'm some conspiracy theorist, it's insulting."

"Don't act like I'm some country rube!"

"You're no rube," I said, "but you've screwed at least one thing up royally. You've got a wolf in the henhouse." I slapped Leachman's file onto his desk, anger stirring in my gut like a storm. "Seems as if I'm not the only one being a fuck-up, eh?"

"What's this?"

"Proof that you're no fool, but you've had your head up your ass."

He opened the file, his eyes fluttering over the paper. "What is this?" he asked. "Where'd you get–"

"Don't worry about that," I said, trying to calm down. "Worry about how that guy's been screwing you and what you're gonna do about it."

"Why did you bring it to me?"

"Because we're both fighting the good fight," I said. "And if you're anything like me, it's nice to know that you're not doing it alone. Sometimes we get blindsided, and when we do, it's nice to remember that not every blindside is bad. I'm here to *help you*."

"How can you help?"

"Let my friends and I lighten your load. You don't need to fight this fight alone."

"This right here is proof that I do," he said, closing the file. "Apparently I can't even trust my own boys."

"Then trust me," I said. "*Please*."

"You've been looking into me, haven't you?"

"What?"

"You think I'm dirty, or you did."

"How do you–"

"You come in here, acting noble and true, but you're just trying to make us look bad. I'm gonna find those two kids, buddy. Trust me, I will. And I don't need help from some paranoid city cop with a big bankroll and powerful connections. You want me out of this, you're gonna have to go to the governor and get me removed, because you ain't getting me off this case. Now get the hell out of here."

He stood and tossed my file at me. It hit my chin, the paper raining down onto the floor. On some level, I understood his anger. On another, I found it the most stubborn and ridiculous thing.

Slowly, I stood.

"When you change your mind, you can find me at the Henlopen," I said, scribbling my phone number on one of the papers from my file and dropping it onto his desk. "You're not dropping this case? Good. Those kids need all the help they can get. But if you think I'm gonna just walk away, you're out of your goddamned mind. I'm going to keep looking, keep asking questions, and keep doing whatever's in my power to do. I don't care if you're insulted or pissed off or what. There are bigger things at stake here than pride. So no, I'm not gonna stop. So you better get used to seeing me around, because I'm not goin' anywhere."

I turned to leave and stopped. "Oh, and Sheriff? God help you if you get in my way."

CHAPTER 19. THE HURDY GURDY MAN

The sun was setting, and we were nowhere.

Red, white, and blue balloons and ribbons festooned the boardwalk, and there was already a healthy crowd gathering for the promised fireworks. The forecast was spotty, our first bit of good luck in days.

Earlier that morning, Clarissa had told me that July's full moon was sometimes called the Thunder Moon on account of storm season and the likelihood for thunder showers. Standing beneath the pavilion at the end of Rehoboth Avenue, I prayed to whatever gods who'd listen that it would storm like hell. If we could somehow buy ourselves two more weeks, we might just have a chance.

Kids ran past, laughing and smiling. Parents walked slowly, holding hands and shaking their heads. Everything smelled like sunscreen and taffy, and if I didn't know any better, I might actually be looking forward to the evening.

In my pocket, a cheap radio crackled. "*Red 1 to Red 2, come in Red 2.*"

I pulled a Gil-approved plastic camo-patterned walkie-talkie out of my pocket. "Gil," I said, "this channel is clear, you can just call me Dylan."

"*Copy, Red 2. What is your location? Over.*"

"I'm at the pavilion."

"*Red 1 copies. Red 1's location is outside the bumper cars. Over.*"

"Where's Finch?"

"*Red 3 is by that kite store. Over.*"

"*As a matter of fact,*" Finch squawked over the line, "*Red 3 is on the move. Making rounds.*"

"And Clarissa?"

"*Pink 1 is... uhhh...*"

"*I'm outside the Sands,*" Clarissa said. "*Should I be moving? Or should I stay still?*"

I held the walkie up to my mouth and froze. Here I was, the only trained cop, and I had no clue what was the best way to tackle the current situation. We were grossly understaffed, and no matter how we coordinated, we were a lot like a blind outfielder trying to catch a pop fly: it could happen, but the odds were not in our favor.

Finally I said, "Keep moving, keep watching. If you see someone you recognize from the case, walkie immediately."

"*Pink 2 here,*" Willa called. "*And can I just say that I really resent my call sign?*"

"*Noted,*" Gil said. "*What's your 20?*"

"*What?*"

"He means where are you?" I said.

"*I am walking past the fire station on Rehoboth Avenue, heading east towards the ocean.*"

"What's foot traffic like on the street?" I asked.

167

"*It was light*," she said, "*but it's really picking up.*"

I checked my watch. "Sunset in about fifty minutes," I said. "Everyone keep moving, and keep your eyes peeled, remember–"

"What the hell are you doing, buddy?" a voice interrupted me.

I turned and found Ponytail facing me.

"My unlucky penny," I said. "Don't you have someone else to annoy?"

The jerk smirked and lifted a pair of purple reflective Oakley's sunglasses. "Playin' cops and robbers?"

"Something like that."

"*Red 2, come in Red 2!*" my walkie screeched.

"Sounds like your Dad is worried," he chuckled.

I sighed. "He's not my Dad–"

"*Red 2!*"

I held the walkie up to my mouth. "Standby," I said, annoyed.

Ponytail's chubby daughter ran up and tugged on his hand, pulling him in the direction of an arcade. Her face was happy, and I couldn't help but worry.

"Hold on, baby," he said, looking down at his daughter. When he looked back up at me, he said, "This guy is–"

"Listen," I interrupted. "You should get out of here. Take your wife and daughter and get out of here."

"Are you threatening–"

"I'm... well, I'm working with the police and they think something bad could happen here." I looked at the young girl pulling excitedly on her jackass Dad's hand, smiling, dreams of winning big at the crane game or the fish pond in her eyes. "Please," I said. "Just listen to me. I'm here to help out, but I don't know what's going to happen. Please, do what I say. Get your family out of here."

"You ain't workin' with the police usin' that radio!" he laughed, pointing at the plastic walkie in my hand.

"Well, I'm–"

The big guy laughed and said, "Come on babygirl." He lifted his daughter and held her close. "Want Poppy to win you a big stuffed bear? Comin' right up!"

He turned and sauntered off.

I cursed and watched helplessly as the two disappeared into the crowd.

In my hand, my walkie crackled. "*Red 2?*"

"False alarm," I said into the small mic. "Keep up the patrols. Everyone keep moving and stay in touch."

I turned and looked up Rehoboth Avenue as the sun continued its slow descent.

Night was falling.

***

I walked south on the boardwalk, passing pizza places and arcades, photo booths and carnival games. Children were everywhere, with half of them running around without a parent in sight. On my left, white benches sat at the boardwalk's edge overlooking the beach and beyond it the ocean. Every bench was filled, the parents saving seats for the big show. In the distance, bobbing up and down on the tide against its anchor, was the long black shape of the fireworks barge. It wouldn't be long now.

I walked through arcades, passing swarms of sunburned kids, some holding cheap prizes, some ice cream cones or Thrasher's french fries with vinnegar. It would be hard enough to patrol the boardwalk alone, but the menagerie of shops and arcades made the task feel insurmountable. The shops were small and cramped; the arcades were poorly lit and full of strobing neon lights from video games.

Past a long row of arcades and pizza joints was Funland, a big stucco building housing the board-walk's contingent of rides. Families bustled in and out, smaller children carried or pushed in strollers towards the haunted house or spinning teacups. I wound through the concourse, passing ticket windows with lines ten deep, fighting for space the whole way. The place was packed. My eyes moved over each face, pausing for only the briefest of moments before moving on to the next. I saw no one I recognized.

Passing something called the *Gravitron*, I bumped into a child, feeling the wet slap of a dropped pizza slice against my leg.

"Ugh, what the–"

I looked down and saw Gil's kite friend scowling at the dropped pizza.

"Sorry, kid," I said. "That was probably my fault.

I'm distracted."

He looked up at me and said something, but in the crowded space, his voice was carried away.

"What?"

"I said, I know you."

"Yeah, my friend showed you how to fly a kite. And I think we saw you again at that diner."

"Yeah."

"Sorry about your pizza," I said.

He looked back at the slice laying face down on the pavement.

"Here," I said, pulling some cash from my back pocket, my arm grazing against the butt of my hidden .38 as I did. "Take some cash. Sorry about that. Buy another."

The kid took a ten. "Thanks."

"What was your name again?"

"Jim."

"Jim," I said. "Listen. Are you here with your parents?"

"They're here somewhere. I think the haunted house."

"You should go home," I said. "Or back to your hotel or whatever."

"Why?"

"It's, uh... It's complicated. But I don't think it's safe here."

He looked at the ten in his hand. "Yeah, okay. Sure." He looked up at me, a little wary and a little annoyed. "See ya."

"All right," I said. "Are you gonna–" I stopped when he slipped away. "See ya," I said. He had disappeared before I could say another word.

Okay, so we hadn't exactly taken to the rooftops to scream warnings, but would you listen if a stranger warned of danger at a Fourth of July event? Maybe in this day and age some people would, but I guess I don't have a creepy enough face to merit caution. People just dismiss me as a paranoid wahoo, apparently.

I walked out of Funland, squeezing past the endless line at the bumper cars and stepped back out onto the boardwalk where I finally saw someone I recognized.

Deputy Carter of the Rehoboth Beach PD. He stood beside a trashcan, speaking quickly into a walkie handset he had clipped to his uniform. His eyes were locked on me.

"Shit," I muttered, trying to slip into the crowd and disappear. Unfortunately, it's a little easier for a skinny kid to hide in a crowd than it is for me. I was six inches taller than almost everyone and about 50 pounds heavier.

I put my head down and plowed forward. In my pocket, I heard my radio crackle. When I pulled it out, it was silent. That was when I realized–

"Hey there," a voice beside me said.

I looked up as the radio squawked again. Only then did I realize it wasn't my radio, it was the Sheriff's.

"What do you want?"

"What are you doing here?"

"Just enjoying the evening," I said. "The fireworks will be starting soon."

He took my arm and lead me out of the crowd to the edge of the boardwalk. "You know what I mean," he said. "What are you *doing* here?"

"Just walking around," I said, shaking his hand off me. "Thinking about getting a hot dog. Why aren't you doing your job?"

"I am doing my job," he said. "Looking out for suspicious characters. The only one I've seen so far is *you.*"

"I'm the least of your worries, Huggins."

"I'm not worried—"

Behind us, a *pop-pop-pop-pop-pop* of cheap fireworks erupted on the boardwalk, clearing a wide circle of passersby and kicking up a billowing cloud of smoke. A few young children screamed. The Sheriff's hand immediately moved to the pistol on his hip.

My hand went for my .38, and he noticed immediately.

"What have you got there?" he asked, reaching for my gun.

I caught his hand and pulled it away. "I'm licensed," I said, reaching for my wallet.

"Hold it," he said, closing his hand around his pistol and grabbing my wrist. "Nice and easy," he said.

"Would you relax? It's my wallet. Good God, man. I think we both have bigger things to worry about than–"

"Don't tell me my business," he said angrily.

"What about your deputy? Donnelly? Is he here, too?"

"No, he was relieved of his duties this morning," Huggins said. "It's just me and Carter now."

"That's the best news I've heard all day."

"I don't know where you–"

The Sheriff's walkie cracked, coming to life and interrupting him mid-sentence. He grabbed the handset clipped to his shoulder. "Go for me," he said.

A static-filled voiced called something back that I couldn't understand. Apparently Huggins couldn't either.

"What? Standby, I can't hear a damn thing." He clicked the radio off and pointed at my face. "You get outta here, you hear me? Go home, go back to Philly, or just plain go to hell. Either way, get outta my town, got me?"

"What did I tell you, Sheriff? I'm not goin' anywhere. I'm going to solve this thing."

He shook his head and bit his lip. "Carter's gonna watch you," he said. "And the public safety guys are on the lookout for you, too. They're gonna be gum on your shoe until you beat it." He turned and waved some signal at Carter who stood about twenty yards away, watching. The Deputy nodded.

"So as long as you're here," the Sheriff said, "I'll be wasting my resources on you. If you care about what's been happening, you'll beat it."

"We'll see," I said. "But don't hold your breath."

He shook his head and lumbered off, speaking into his radio once he was out of earshot.

"Gil," I said into my radio. "We got problems."

"*If you're talkin' about the guys with police tees and short shorts, Red 2, I'm way ahead of you*," Gil said immediately. "*Two goons on bicycles have been following me for twenty minutes.*"

I gritted my teeth and bit back a few choice words I would've liked to share with Sheriff Huggins. "Just... just do your best to lose them. If you can't, just ignore them and keep moving around, keep looking." I looked over my shoulder and saw Deputy Carter's shape. "It's what I'm gonna do. We have to. It's all we can do."

***

I walked around with Carter for a few minutes before I lost him in a tee shirt store, slipping out the back entrance and into a funnel cake stand's kitchen and then back out the front. Sun finally got below the horizon, dropping the boardwalk into shadow. Slowly, the arcades began to empty as people moved towards the beach. I watched the sky, waiting for the storm that would save the day. Dark clouds were gathering, but there was no storm yet.

I continued the patrol. As it got darker, I became more aware of black clothes, even going so far as to stop a few goth teens I saw harassing kids behind a shell shop. I pulled the kids loose from whatever ass-kicking they were about to get and sent the bullies packing.

Back on the boardwalk, darkness had fallen. Above, the stars were fighting to come out. Fighting and losing. Without any sun, I couldn't see dark clouds, but a flash of lightning in the distance was promising.

From a PA system somewhere, a voice came to life. "*Ladies and gentlemen, please make your way to the boardwalk. The fireworks will begin in five minutes!*"

An excited murmur passed through the crowd as walkers began to slow and take their places on the board walk, further congesting the already bustling space.

Fear began setting in. I saw hints of the black figure everywhere: silhouetted against the neon of a Grotto's Pizza sign, lurking behind the animatronic fortune teller *Zoltar*, slinking across the sand towards the surf. At one point, I grabbed a tall guy wearing a black windbreaker, apologizing for the confusion as I let him go.

"Anybody have eyes on *anything*?" I asked the radio angrily. Worse than being ineffectual was feeling like you were wasting your time. I'd seen nothing, and I felt like we may as well not even be out there. With each man or woman I incorrectly stopped, I felt more and more certain that a child was being taken somewhere else.

"*Nothing,*" Finch said.

"*Same,*" Willa called.

"*No, not a thing,*" Clarissa added.

"Gil?"

"*Nada, big man,*" he finally added with a sigh. "*Is that a good thing or a–*"

Above us, thunder rumbled, long and slow and patiently. It sounded like it came from over the ocean. I waited and a flash of lightning followed.

"I'd say that there is a good thing. Will they cancel?" I asked. "Do you think they–"

"*Ladies and Gentlemen, please proceed to the boardwalk. The fireworks will begin in two minutes!*" the voice on the PA intoned.

It didn't take a genius to realize that fireworks were the best distraction a kidnapper could ask for. Everyone would simultaneously look upward, ignoring everything but the spectacle out over the ocean. To make matters worse, a lot of businesses tended to turn out their lights for the show. We had to find a way to stop it.

"Gil," I said. "Do you think we can call something in? Something to stop the show?"

"*Like what?*" he asked. "*We've got two minutes! And I don't think I'm prepared to cause widespread panic to–*"

"*Ladies and gentlemen, welcome to the Rehoboth Beach Fourth of July celebration!*" the announcer said over the PA.

A smattering of applause rippled across the crowd.

"You're right," I said. "I've been... damnit, everyone take a step back," I said, my mind racing. "Get off the boardwalk, look behind you. The board-walk is too crowded. Look where no one else is looking. Attention is going to be focused at the ocean. Turn around and backtrack—"

"*Our annual fireworks extravaganza will begin shortly, celebrating our nation's independence!*"

I started walking backwards, my mind finally working. It was as if my training had taken a nap and was just beginning to stir. "Alleyways, arcades, Funland, we need to look in places that are being vacated. Get off the boardwalk!"

Overhead, thunder rumbled again, this time closer. A flash of lightning lit the night sky. An awed *ooooooh* rose from the crowd. An old man to my left shouted, "Hurry up, start the show!"

I moved back, pushing my way through parents as I felt drops of rain on my bare skin. "Come on," I urged. "*Rain!*"

I rushed into the nearest arcade, finding it almost completely empty. Winding my way through racing consoles and crane games, I almost smiled when I found not one child. If only they were all like this—

"*Dylan,*" Willa called over the walkie. "*They're turning the lights out down here!*"

I realized we didn't have flashlights and cursed the oversight. "Keep looking, it's almost time! If it's going to happen, it's—"

Over the PA, Ray Charles' "America the Beautiful" started to play. All around me, neon lights began to go out, storefronts closing their doors and extinguishing their lights in preparation for the fireworks.

"*Here too,*" Gil said. "*Funland is dark!*"

"Damnit," I said, shaking my head. "We're out of time..."

A flash of lightning lit a storm-marbled sky. At that moment, a streak of red launched from the barge, lancing straight into the sky and erupting in a brilliant red, white, and blue explosion over the ocean. The crowd began to cheer as Ray Charles carried through the first verse of "America the Beautiful."

I pushed through the crowd, moving in a line parallel to the ocean, towards the next bank of arcades. Above me, a crash of thunder overwhelmed the pounding of fireworks and music. Three flashes of lightning followed immediately.

That's when the rain started.

In the semi-darkness, I couldn't claim the rain as a victory, not anymore. It was too dark to see as it was, and when the flood of water came pouring down, visibility dropped to almost nil. Waves of people turned and withdrew into the cover of the once empty arcades in a stampede, emptying the boardwalk in a flash. On the distant barge, the fireworks continued, tiny sparks firing up into the sky and exploding in kaleidoscopes of color. I huddled beside an ATM as waves of people pushed past me.

Ray Charles continued as I pushed back out onto the suddenly empty boardwalk. The music was drowned out as another crash of thunder ripped through the sky. It was a lot to handle, but in the pit of my stomach, I suddenly felt a sick knot of stress twist and tighten. In the pouring rain, I closed my eyes and extended my senses outwards, feeling for the faintest hint of magical power.

And I felt it. It whipped across me like a hay-maker.

The rain fell in sheets, but through the darkness, I saw a slow, rickety, unnatural movement slide through the night like a walking shadow. It stumbled up over the dunes, walking away from the ocean. Above, a burst of fireworks exploded, casting a pale green light over the dark shape.

It was the witch.

I turned and ran towards it. From behind me, I heard a voice shout, but I ignored it. The shape crossed the boardwalk, still rickety, but picking up speed, streaking across the wet boards. Too fast, I slipped on the slick surface and fell. Cursing, I climbed to my feet and took off once again, shouting into my radio, "*I got it! Past Funland and moving down a side street. I need everybody now!*"

I passed Funland, and I took a screeching right turn down Brooklyn Avenue. Halfway down the block I saw a narrow back entrance to Funland, little more than a spillway to additional street parking. A short shape was lifted from where it stood, the dark figure barely slowing.

I heard a scream. A child's scream.

"No!" I shouted. "Goddamn you, I see you and I'm coming, you son of a bitch!"

I picked up speed, fury building in my gut as my emotions unleashed the power of the vael.

Unnatural power flowed through me, and I began to move faster, the fatigue in my muscles burning off. Above me, lightning flashed, mixing in with fireworks, illuminating the street. In the bright white light, I saw the tiny shape, writhing and struggling against the witch as I closed the distance between us.

I touched the black cloak, my hand closing over it as I planted my feet and dug in, scrambling to a stop. Legs tangled and I rolled forward. The cloth pulled and tore, and the rickety shape in front of me seemed to crumble along with me. A child's scream punctuated the fall, and I saw a young girl tumble to the ground.

Lightning flashed and illuminated the witch's profile. A long, sharp nose came off her face like a knife. Above it, two blank, unnatural disc eyes stared, unseeing.

Cloak still knotted in my hand, I fought against the witch, the thin body surprisingly strong, one arm still locked around the child. I swung my free hand out, clenched in a fist, slamming it across the witch's face.

The face came off and spiraled to the ground.

It wasn't a face, it was a mask fashioned from cloth and metal.

"Oh my God."

A gunshot erupted behind me, the bullet zipping over my head and burying itself in the trunk of a nearby tree. Overhead, another crash of thunder split the sky. I neither saw the bullet nor heard the thunder, my eyes were locked on the witch.

Only then did I realize it wasn't a witch. We'd been wrong about everything.

Beneath the mask was nothing, no face at all. Only a skull, bleached white and lifeless, a pair of empty sockets for eyes and wide lipless mouth of teeth grinning at me in death.

Shouting continued, but it meant nothing.

"But... oh Jesus... you're–"

Another gunshot, this one closer. The shouting voice continued, but I was frozen, my muscles locked and unable to move.

Only when the child screamed did I come back to life.

"Let her go, you–"

The gun sounded once more and the bullet passed through my chest in a spray of blood. My hand spasmed, releasing the cloak. Blood poured from my chest, mixing with the torrential rain and puddling beneath me.

The skeleton rose slowly to its feet, its movements once more rickety and unnatural. It took a step back and began to drift away, disappearing into the rain and darkness, carrying the child.

Behind me, I still heard the shouting, the voice getting nearer and nearer. Only when the skeleton was gone did I turn, slowly and painfully. "What are you–"

Deputy Donnelly, aka William Leachman, stood over me, breathlessly pointing his pistol at my temple. "You sold me out," he panted. "You ruined every-thing, you bastard! You gave the Sheriff my file–"

Before he could finish, Gil slammed into him, sending him headfirst into the grill of a parked pickup truck.

I coughed and tasted blood. Gil was at my side, saying my name over and over, but I couldn't speak.

The rain sounded like a mocking round of applause. Thunder rumbled.

I put my head down on the pavement and closed my eyes.

CHAPTER 20. AGE OF TREASON

It was still raining when I opened my eyes and stared into a blinding light.

"I'm not dead," I said. "Am I in the hospital?"

"No," Gil said. "Welcome back to the land of the–"

"Turn off that goddamn light."

"Okay."

The light clicked off.

I blinked about a dozen times and Gil came into focus. He had a sad droop to his world-weary brown eyes. We were sitting in one of the penthouse's bedrooms.

"How you feelin', big man?"

My left arm was in a sling across my chest. A layering of bandages wound tightly around my chest and shoulder, and I felt like a freshly-wrapped mummy.

"Pretty good, actually," I said softly. "Thirsty, though."

Gil handed me a glass of water that sat on a bedside table. I took a deep gulp.

"Sorry the gang's not here to greet you," he said. "They're... busy."

"That's all right," I sighed. The window to my left was dark and spattered with raindrops. "Are they looking for–"

"Yeah," Gil said.

"Who was it?"

"A girl named Allison Brady."

I nodded, staring out the window. After a moment, I turned to Gil. "Brady?"

He met my gaze sullenly. "Uh huh. It's just who you think."

"That guy I punched?"

He nodded. "His little kid."

"Didn't we see her–"

He nodded. "At the diner that day. She wore the Wonder Woman shirt."

I looked back out the window. Physically, I felt remarkably good. In every other way I felt horrible.

"What time is it?"

"3:30AM," Gil said. "You've been out for almost six hours."

I pulled the sheet back and moved my legs, a deep, aching pain creeping through my chest. I groaned.

"Hold it there, big man," Gil said. "You may have gotten lucky, but–"

"This isn't luck," I said. "I've been shot before."

"All right, so Hanas used the word 'miraculous,' but you know that pesky vael–"

"No internal damage?" I asked as I continued my slow climb back to my feet.

Gil shook his head. "No. Like I said, 'miraculous.'"

I dropped my bare feet onto the carpet and took a deep breath. It felt like I was breathing fire. I let it out slowly and felt woozy.

Still, as a gunshot to the chest goes, this was a walk in the park.

I stood upright, a little uneasy on my feet before I steadied.

"What are you–"

I walked past him slowly. "We have work to do, remember?"

***

In the penthouse's great room, there was arguing.

"But I don't believe it *was* worth it, Finch!" Willa said, exasperated.

"It was a worthy gamble," Finch replied. "We had no way of knowing that–"

"If we had no idea it would shake down like that, then we were fools."

"That remains to be seen," Finch said, his voice measured. "The game has not ended yet."

"What are you arguing about?" I asked. "Can't you see you've woken me?"

"Dylan!" Willa said. "What are you–"

"I think Boss said something about a miracle or whatever?" I shook my head. "What's the story?"

"We've been trying to get on this, but we're not

making much progress. You shouldn't be up!"

"No," Finch said. "We need to debrief you–"

"No," Willa interrupted. "He needs rest. He can't be–"

"That's enough," I said angrily. "I'm not fine, but I'm okay to keep moving. If you think I'm going to get back in that bed, you're out of your mind. And remember: miraculous healing. Don't worry about me. Worry about the girl." I turned to Gil. "What was her name?"

"Allison Brady."

"Allison Brady," I repeated. "So what happened?"

"The Sheriff was here," Willa said. "He gave us a brief rundown."

"Apparently, he relieved Deputy John Donnelly from duty at approximately two o'clock this afternoon."

"Was he arrested?"

Finch shook his head. "The Sheriff had no grounds for arrest. He contacted the Iowa PD, but had yet to receive a call back by the time he departed the station for the Independence Day festivities."

"And this guy... what? You think he came there tonight to kick my ass?"

"It would seem," Finch said. "We know the police were previously alerted of your presence as well as Gil's. And we know that Deputy Donnelly saw your face at least once. There is also a good chance he was at the station while you had your meeting with the Sheriff."

I thought back to my shouting in Huggins' office. I'd been foolish not to practice even *minimal* discretion.

"So he came tonight and saw me. Do I chalk his attack up to bad timing?"

Finch shrugged. "Of that, I am not certain."

"I don't think so," Gil said. "You can't."

I looked at Willa. "What do you think?"

"I think that's just too coincidental."

"What happened to Donnelly after I was shot?"

"The Sheriff apprehended him. He is currently locked up at the police station."

"And... am I the only one who saw the... the thing in black?"

There was silence. Everyone looked at me, waiting.

"Really?" I asked. "Gil, come on. You had to see something."

"I saw... just the shape, but that was it. I didn't see her face or–"

"It's not a witch," I said. "I don't know much, but it wasn't a witch. It was... a skeleton."

"Um? Whaddya mean?"

"I knocked a... well, a mask off. We were fighting and I hit it. It was dark, but I saw that it was a mask when I hit it and it came off."

"What did the mask look like?" Finch asked.

"It was..." I closed my eyes, visualizing the strange face. "The eyes were perfect circles. Large. Too large to be natural. They were black. The nose...

the nose was long, really long and pointed. I can see why people thought it was witchy."

"Almost like a bird?" Finch asked, a faint light of recognition in his eyes. He stepped over to the kitchen table and turned Willa's laptop to face him. "Excuse me," he said softly, "do you mind if I–?"

"No, not at all."

"Definitely like a bird," I said. "The eyes were almost like lenses. They–"

"If I can..." Finch trailed off, typing slowly. He frowned. "How do I?" he looked up at Willa. "The internet utility?"

She smiled sadly and helped him with the computer.

After a minute, he turned the computer around. "Like this?" he said.

I found myself staring at an old engraving of the creature. The image showed a tall figure in a long robe, a walking stick in hand. Beneath a wide-brimmed hat was the strange avian face, complete with long beak and round, empty eyes.

"My God," I said, a chill tiptoeing up my spine. "That's it. That's what I saw. What the hell is that?"

"It was called a Plague Doctor," Finch said. "And it's most commonly associated with the Black Death, also known as the Bubonic Plague."

"Oh," I said, my mouth hanging open slightly. "That's... good to know."

"I can tell you more," he said. "But I need to do research. I need to check a few things. It could be..." He trailed off and shook his head. After a moment, he turned the laptop back to Willa, thanking her quietly before he rushed off to his room.

Gil took a seat at the kitchen table. "The plague," he said quietly, staring off into space.

Willa licked her lips and took a deep breath. "Dylan," she said. "Can I talk to you for a second?" She gestured out of the great room, meaning she wanted to speak alone.

"*Oooh*," Gil said. "Willa and Dylan, sittin' in a–"

I scowled at him and he shut up. Slowly, I followed her out onto a covered balcony. She pulled the sliding glass door behind us. I watched the rain fall over the empty boardwalk.

"What is it?" I asked.

"While you were out, I took Gil's advice, I started expanding my financial searches–"

"Is this really important?" I interrupted. "Finch just used the words 'Black Death' in a practical, concrete sense. I don't know how important bank accounts are right now."

"Just listen, please," she said. "I started checking more financial records. I checked City Council. I checked the other Deputy. I checked–"

I took a breath and it hurt. "Get to it," I said, my ire rising. "I feel awful and–"

"Jane," she said. "Jane Julius. That's her name, right?"

"She said it wasn't, no–"

"I know. I found her. I found the *real* her. And she's been lying to you. She's been lying all along."

If my ire had been rising, at that moment it

decided to take flight. "She's been lying about half a dozen things, Willa. Why are you obsessing over this? Because a girl was kidnapped tonight, and there are better things–"

"I'm worried, Dylan, *and* I'm doing what I was asked to do. This isn't about me. Goddamn, is that what you think? It's about all of us, and it's about that girl. If we can't figure out what this is really about, then she is going to die and it'll be on us. This girl and the other two kids who were taken."

I gritted my teeth. "All right, what is she lying about?"

"The book," she said. "She's lying about the book. The grimoire, that dangerous book that she stole?"

"The one powerful enough to summon evil hell creatures from other dimensions and that may actually be able to unleash the Devil himself? I remember it, yeah."

"She never sold it."

"She what? Gil said she sold it to a guy named Roach–"

"Finch told me Jane said she was *paid* to steal it. She said she stole the book and sold it for a lot of money, right?" Willa shook her head. "She didn't. The Roach buyer must have been a false leak. There was never any money, no huge deposits were made; *that was her lie*. She still has that grimoire. And she just happens to show up here when all this is going straight to hell?" Willa shook her head again. "No way. She never did anything with it; she stole it for *herself*. She's got the book and she's here for a reason, and it doesn't take a rocket scientist to put two and two together. She's behind this, Dylan. She's been behind everything."

CHAPTER 21. BELATED FORGIVENESS PLEA

Below the great red *Dolly's* sign that overlooked the boardwalk at the terminus of Rehoboth Avenue, I was standing under the overhang, waiting.

After speaking with Willa, I'd called Jane on the number she'd left me. To my surprise, she answered. She shocked me further by agreeing to meet.

For an arch enemy, she seemed quite agreeable.

And so here I stood, out of the rain, but wet from the walk. The boardwalk was deserted–as you'd expect it to be at 4AM–but the street lights running the length of the boardwalk were lit. Amber halos of light shone down on the wet wooden esplanade. I waited and watched, but there was no one in sight.

"Why did you call me?"

I turned. Somehow she had snuck up behind me, even though my back had been to the building.

"Not for a screw, if that's what you thought."

"It's not," she said. "If it was, I would have ignored you."

"Nice."

"What do you want?"

"Why are you in Rehoboth?"

"Are you serious? You called me out here at 4AM to ask me the question you've asked five times already? Do you really think my answer will be different–"

"I know about the book," I said.

Her face was stony, her eyes suspicious.

"What do you mean?"

"I know that you never sold it. And if I gave a shit, I could know your last name. I didn't get that far though. I didn't care to."

"What about the book?"

"You have it–"

"I *don't* have it."

"Don't lie to me."

"I sold the book, Dylan."

"I said *don't lie to me*–"

"I'm not lying!"

"We saw your goddamn bank records. We looked at everything. If you sold the book, you sold it for chickenshit, not the fortune you said–"

"I could have hidden the money–"

"You didn't. You didn't *get* any money, Jane."

"You think you know everything about me? What makes you think you know *anything*?"

"I know enough." I was just about yelling now, my voice easily carrying over the rain. Anger was quickly filling me. "I know you're a liar and that I can't trust you for shit."

"I'm telling you, I don't have the book."

"Maybe not here, but you've got it."

"I don't, I swear–"

"Save it, Jane," I said. "Just save it. You told me that you had nothing to do with the kidnappings. Nothing. But still, you're here. Why? What are you doing here?"

"I told you, I was–"

"Don't say looking at property or vacationing or whatever. It's insulting. Do you really think that little of me?"

"I'm beginning to, yeah."

"You want me to trust you? How? What can I trust? You've told me nothing true."

"I've told you plenty–"

"Like what?"

"I don't have the goddamn book!"

"You didn't sell it, so where is it?"

"Just because I didn't sell it doesn't mean I still have it."

"So you admit you lied?"

"*Everyone* lies about money," she said. "But that's all. I don't have the book."

"What did you do with it?"

"I was hired to steal it–"

"–yeah–"

"–and I stole it."

"–yeah–"

"And... then I gave it up."

"–you gave it up?"

"Traded it."

"You traded it?"

She turned away, sighing loudly. "Damnit, it's... complicated."

"Fucking talk to me, Jane. What is going on? What are you doing here? And what do you know?"

"Why? You think you're my friend? You came here tonight to accuse me–"

"I came here tonight for the truth. I came to level with you and give you a chance to level with me."

"Level with you about what?"

"The book. This is all about the book, isn't it? It's too much of a coincidence, otherwise. Your being here, I mean."

"There aren't any coincidences in this business," she said. "Haven't you learned that yet?"

"What do you mean?"

"I'm here *because* of the book."

"What?"

She shook her head. "You think I'm some stone cold bitch, Dylan, that I sold the book for a profit."

"Well, you told us–"

"I had to give it up," she said. "I *had* to."

"Give it up to who?"

"You don't know him–"

"It was Carrion, wasn't it?"

I'd interrupted her, and her mouth was open. When I said his name, she froze. The only sound I heard for a long while was the sound of the rain, hard and steady.

"What did you say?" she finally asked.

"Carrion," I said. "You gave it to Carrion."

"How do you know about him?"

Slowly, I shook my head. "I've met him," I said. "And he's a bastard."

"I know," she said. "I know exactly what he is. You guys really thought I *profited* off that damn book? That I *wanted* to steal it?"

"You told us—"

"I *lied*. I told you what I had to tell you to make it through that night alive, to make it through with the damn book."

"Why didn't you level with us? Why didn't you tell us? We could have helped you, we could have—"

"You don't know him," she said.

I shook my head. Oh, little did she know.

She continued, "The Battery? They are the Empire State and you guys are three ants. You could've helped me? How? No, really, *how*?"

"We could... we could have thought of something together—"

She shook her head. "I did what I had to do because I am under contract to them, Dylan, I *had* to do it. They don't give you choices. And because of that, I had to come here, I had to see what I could do to help undo what I'd done—"

"What? What do you mean?"

"I... I don't know much," she admitted. "But I know the kidnappings have to do with the book." She sighed. "You were right. This is all about the book."

"The thing in black," I said. "Do you know what it is? Do you—"

"The Plague Doctor?"

My breath caught in my throat. "...yes."

"Someone is using the book to control it, to *conjure* it. There may even be more than one. It... *they* came from the book, Dylan."

"How do you know?"

"That book is priceless, and I had it in my possession for four days before I turned it over. Do you really think I didn't look through the whole thing?"

"What did you learn?" I asked. "Tell me; we have to know because—"

"The kids," she said, nodding. "That's why I'm here; that's why I'm telling you all of this. It's not because of you, it's... it's not what you think. I'm here because I can't just leave knowing they're gone. I'm not sorry for taking it. I did what I had to do for *me*. Do you understand that? But I'm sorry about what's happened since. I'm sorry about the kids. I didn't know this was going to happen."

"I believe you—"

"So I came here to help. I was there yesterday," she said. "I was on the boardwalk when that girl was taken, I was trying to prevent it, too. But I was on the opposite end. I guessed wrong about where it might happen. But you almost stopped it—"

"Tell me what you know, Jane."

She took a deep breath, finally raising her eyes to mine, and told me everything she knew. It wasn't much, but it was enough.

When she was done, she was silent. I opened my

mouth, ready to tell her that I understood her predicament all too well, that I too was under contract to the Battery. I too was just a pawn, the smallest cog in their huge machine.

The words were on the tip of my tongue, and looking into her rain-drenched and sullen face, I still couldn't do it. Maybe I was angry. Maybe I was exhausted. Maybe it was both, but all I could say was, "Thanks."

With that, I turned away and trudged back into the rain, leaving her behind, my fresh bullet wound aching with each step. One more scar to add to the bunch.

CHAPTER 22. THE WAR DRAGS ON

When I walked in the door, Willa was at the computer, eyes locked on her laptop screen. Finch sat across from her, a half-dozen books spread open in front of him. Outside of the kitchen, I could see Gil pacing, his lit pipe locked in his teeth.

"It's the Battery," I said.

"What?" Gil shouted from across the room. "Did you just say what I think you just said?"

"Yeah. It's the Battery. Jane... *sold* the book to the Battery."

Willa looked up. "But what about–"

"She sold it," I said, catching her eye. "How isn't important. But she did."

"It isn't that I don't believe her," Finch said, "although I don't, as a matter of fact. But why would they do this? For what purpose–"

"She knows... not a lot about that," I admitted. "But she pointed me in the right direction."

"What direction was that?" Gil asked.

"Do you know what something called *metempsychosis* is?"

Gil took his pipe from his mouth and said, "Ummmm–"

"It can't be," Finch interrupted, shaking his head. "I thought about that, Dylan, but it simply cannot be the case."

"Palingenesia?" I said. "That's the same thing, right? I spoke with Jane–"

"She is mistaken," Finch said, shaking his head.

"–and I'm beginning to think this is all about that damn book." I looked at Willa. "I think you were right about that."

"What book again?" Gil asked.

"The grimoire," I said.

"*My* grimoire?" Gil asked. "I just write stories in there, stories that are best not shared with–"

"No," Finch interrupted. "Not that book. *The* grimoire. *Y Ddraig Goch*, *The Red Dragon*, *The Grand Grimoire*."

"I thought we weren't supposed to–"

"The book is not near," Finch said. "The name is only powerful when the book is close by."

"My point is, she *read* it."

"She did what?"

"She read the book, the... that grimoire."

"*The Grand Grimoire*?"

"Yes, all right, the–no, I'll just call it *The Red Dragon*."

"I told you, you can call it–"

"I don't want to," I said bitterly. "It's been hammered into my head that we can't call it that. There's no changing it now."

"*Anyway*," Gil said. "What did she read?"

"Specific references to metempsychosis and the means by which it can be accomplished."

"You sound like him," Gil said, aping Finch and his faint accent. "'And the means by which it can be–'"

"It is not true," Finch said, shaking his head. "Metempsychosis and Palingenesia. Those are nothing but legends–"

"Names," I said. "She gave me names. Proof. Ennius and the Count of Saint Germain."

"You are conflating theories," Finch said, sighing. "Ennius was a Roman, learned in the ways of Plato–"

"She said Plato, too!"

Finch continued, unfettered. "–while the *Comte de* Saint Germain claimed to be an alchemist in possession of the elixir of life, two *completely* different ideas–"

"Just let him talk, Finch!" Gil interrupted. He turned to me. "What was the point, big man?"

I took a breath. "She didn't just read about metempsychosis. She read about the means by which it can be... well, how it can be done."

"I can see where this is going," Finch said. "And I do *not* think that–"

"Cut the big words. You're talking... sacrifice?" Gil asked. "As in *human sacrifice*?"

"Not in the classical sense," I said. When I thought of human sacrifice, my mind immediately ran to the Mayans and the Acropolis.

"Not in the classical sense?" Gil asked. "How much do you know about human sacrifice?"

"Not much," I admitted, "but from what Jane could tell me, this is... a little different."

"You are talking about energy," Finch said. He shook his head. "I'm unconvinced that what you are speaking of is even scientifically possible."

"But you explained to me that magic is just otherworld science, right? Science from parallel worlds or alternate realities? Didn't you say that?"

"Well, yes," Finch said, "I did say that, but–"

"Then how can we *know* what's possible? And if we can't disprove it," I said, "and it's all we've got to work on, then don't we need to act as if this is correct? Procedurally, it's our strongest piece of concrete evidence, hell, it's the *only* piece of concrete evidence we've got."

"I do not think an ageless grimoire with questionable origins can be considered a strong piece of concrete evidence," Finch complained.

"He's right," Gil said. "It's... it's all we've got." He turned to me. "What can we use to learn about *this* situation, though? The theories in the book are general, not specific. How can we use the general theories to help us *now*? This is all... what's the word I'm looking for? Academic. If this isn't practical, it's all academic and a waste of time."

"Well... I did learn that the sacrifice has to be made during the lunar third quarter, on a telluric current–"

"Is that like a Ley line?" Gil asked. "Because I dunno what a current thingy is, but I know what a Ley line is..."

"No," Finch said. "A telluric current is different. Telluric currents are naturally occurring electrical fields in the surface of the Earth." He looked at me. "This person is using a lot of natural energy, Dylan. You really believe that he or she intends to–"

"Sacrifice the three children to bring someone back to life?" I nodded. "Yes, I do."

"And you think it is the Battery behind it?"

"It adds up," I said. "Doesn't it? They bought the book from Jane, they have the clout to be tampering with bank records, and they have the resources to funnel big, *big* dollars into people's accounts–"

"But *why*?" Finch asked. "You are forgetting the *why*. The Battery is not fond of the past. You must remember that they are a corporation, they move *forward*. To a corporation, there is no *value* in the past. It is gone."

"There's value if you could bring it back," I said.

After a short silence, Finch nodded. "A fair point, perhaps."

"Okay," I said. "So our next move should be finding the agent of the Battery."

"You mean their man on the ground, right?" Gil asked.

"Yes, exactly. They'll need someone here, acting as their eyes and ears, manipulating the situation–"

"To say nothing of controlling the Plague Doctor," Finch said. "Perhaps you just may have something there."

"That's why we *need* to find the coven," I said. "A group of people who–"

"Guys?" Willa said, clearing her voice. "I don't mean to interrupt your expository brainstorm, but I think I just found something relevant. Something... very relevant."

"What is it?"

"You said someone to be the eyes and ears? Someone to manipulate? Someone who had a grasp of magic?"

"Yeah, so?"

She turned her computer around. "These are phone records," she said. "Over the past two weeks, Clarissa has called the sheriff fifteen times. He has called her nine times."

"She's probably been pestering him for info," I said. "She said she was–"

"No," Finch interrupted. "She did not say anything about that. Ms. Donnegan has not intimated a close relationship with Sheriff Huggins."

I opened my mouth to defend her, but found no words. Clarissa had crept into our case, and rather unassumingly at that. The Sheriff, on the other hand, wanted our meddling selves as far from the case as he could get us. You'd think I'd be mad, but I wasn't. I looked down, my eyes wandering over my wet shoes.

"It doesn't look good," Gil admitted.

"The Plague Doctor did not attack her, did it?" Finch asked. "She was present for the attack, but was never in any danger."

"No," I said softly, "she wasn't."

"All right," Gil said, "let's back up. Did anyone have eyes on her last night?"

We three looked at him silently. "Dylan was closest," he continued, "and I was about a block behind him."

"I saw Finch outside of Funland," Willa said. "We were both haulin' ass after we heard–"

"What about Clarissa?" he interrupted. "Weird for me to say 'let's focus,' but let's focus. Did anyone see Clarissa?"

Their silence told me everything. That sinking feeling in my stomach was worsening.

"Where is she now?" I asked.

"After it was over," Gil said, "she told us she needed to be alone; she said she needed to rest."

"In retrospect," Finch said, "perhaps it was... *unwise* to let her leave."

"Ya think?" I asked, shaking my head. "Now what?"

Finch spoke up, "You said something about the third quarter moon of the lunar–"

"Oh, yeah," I said. "I'd almost forgotten the best news. If this moon stuff is reliable, and it has been so far, it means we have four days."

No one replied. Outside, the sun was up over the ocean, climbing slowly. Gil checked his watch. "I think it's about time we wake some people up."

CHAPTER 23. WHERE IS SHE?

I got the Tank out of the underground garage and we drove the few blocks to Clarissa's house in silence. At that point, I believe we were all thinking Clarissa's hands were dirty.

The trouble with worst-case scenarios is that sometimes, they're not quite clear–or bad–or bad *enough*.

When we got to Clarissa's, the front door was smashed in.

"What the hell is going on?" Gil asked, stepping through the fractured doorframe.

"I don't know," I said, my anger abating. "Either she's jumped town... or someone else came to visit. Boss," I said, jogging up the stairs behind him, "let me go in first!" I pulled my .38 out of my belt with my good arm, leveling the pistol in front of me.

"Why? Do you think someone's here–"

"We don't know *who's* here," I said softly. "So stay behind me."

The waiting room was as it should have been, but Clarissa's "inner sanctum" was not. The small reading table was overturned, the few lava lamps smashed. Her star chart lay torn on the floor.

"Upstairs," I said, gesturing.

Her apartment was much the same. Much of the damage sustained to the second floor was search-related, the great bookcases cleaned out, their collection of books piled unceremoniously on the floor. Other damage was definitely personal. Clarissa's collection of photographs was smashed, the small frames destroyed, the glass in each reduced to little more than powder.

"Someone was looking for something," I said. "But that wasn't it. They wanted to hurt her, to frighten her. Maybe they wanted her to tell them something. Maybe she wasn't even here. Maybe she's on the lam. I... I just don't know."

Gil knelt and lifted a ruined picture of Clarissa and her husband from Disney World. There was a hole in the picture ripped through her husband's chest.

"Who would do this?" he asked, his voice low.

I took a deep breath, relying on my years of experience and professionalism to carry me through the awfulness of the situation.

"Plenty of people," I said, shaking my head. "Bad people. The question is: why? What did they want?"

Gil dropped the picture of the husband, and spiraling to the floor, it caught my eye.

"Wait," I said.

I knelt and picked it up. Something about the husband's face seemed familiar. I'd looked at it the first time I'd visited the apartment, but I'd seen it again. I'd seen it at–

"Son of a bitch," I said.

"What?"

"We were on the wrong track again."

***

Sheriff Huggins was at his desk, his eyes red, dark circles blooming beneath each.

"What is it?" he asked as I pushed open the door.

I lifted the picture I'd found at Clarissa's house. "Who is this?" I asked.

"Where did you get–"

"This is your brother," I said. "And your brother's wife."

After a moment, he nodded.

"Why didn't you tell us?"

"Why would I?"

"All right, why didn't *she* tell us?"

"With all the stuff going on, she didn't want anyone to know," he said. "She thought it would reflect badly on *me*, her being... well, a witch. She wanted to help me, wanted to look into what was happening. I didn't want her to, but she thought she could help."

"You let your brother's widow help, but not guys trained to help?"

He shrugged, an action that looked damn callous given the circumstances.

"What's going on with you?" I asked. "How wrong am I to trust a goddamn thing you say?"

"What?"

"She's gone, maybe on the run, maybe in trouble.

Where were you all last night?"

"Right here!" he said.

"Alone?"

"Well... yeah. Did you say she's gone?"

"Yeah, I did. Probably on the run. I... you..." I tried to put together some kind of accusation, but it just wasn't happening. I was so tired and so at a loss, I didn't even know what to say. "You've been jerking us around since we got here."

"What? No, I haven't–"

"Shut up," I said. "You put on a good front, but you're crooked as the day is long." I shook my head. "I don't trust you, I don't trust anybody. Let me talk to your deputy."

"Carter? He's at home, sleeping–"

"No," I said. "The one that shot me. Donnelly, or whatever."

"He's not here."

"What? Where is he?"

"That FBI guy came," he said. "I didn't hear back from Iowa–"

"You didn't keep him here? You should've charged him with attempted murder!" I gestured at my sling. "I'm shot here! That fucking guy shot me!"

"I couldn't keep him," he said. "Not when the FBI–"

"Who was it?"

"What?"

"Who took him? What was the agent's name?"

"Allagash," he said. "Jonathan Allagash."

I sighed. "Allagash? Are you serious?"

***

"I thought we'd already hit the low point," Gil said.

We were sitting on the balcony, each holding a stiff drink, as the sun set. Another day wasted.

"You can always go lower," Willa said softly.

"Sad but true."

My phone rang. I pulled it out of my pocket and answered. Finch, Gil, and Willa looked at me as I spoke two words and listened. After a moment, I hung up.

"Jane can't find her either. Madame Clarissa is, effectively, gone."

"Credit cards and debit cards are silent," Willa said. "And her car is still parked on the street outside her place."

"Meaning she's been kidnapped, too?" Gil asked.

"Maybe, yeah."

"What about this Agent Allagash?" Finch asked.

"Same thing," Willa said. "No idea where he is or where he's going."

"We're assuming he works for the Battery, right?" I asked.

"Sure?" she said. "No idea."

There it was. No idea. None of us had any clue what was happening. We'd just figured out *why*–probably–but it wasn't helping to narrow down the search. I think I'd just about turned on everybody, accusing them of being the mastermind behind this master plan. So far, I'd been wrong every time.

Gil put down his drink and stood up, turning his back on the ocean. He smiled, his sunburn fading slowly. "How are we doing, gang?"

No one said a word.

"That good, eh? We've really taken a few on the chin, haven't we? I'm gettin' a little tired of it, frankly. But... fear not! I just had an idea."

As one, I think we grumbled something unintelligible.

"No, really," Gil said. "I've got an idea. I think it'll help get the wheels a-turnin', okay?"

* * *

I stood at the tee of the seventeenth hole, miniature putter in hand, red golfball at my feet. Ten yards ahead of me, the green astroturf carpet took a sharp left turn at the base of a seven-foot tall viking statue. The great bearded fellow held a battle ax across his chest and wore one of those horned helmets.

"You know how hard this is to do with one hand?" I asked for about the thirteenth time.

"It's an *exercise*, you fuddy-duddies!" Gil shouted from beside the flag marked **17**. "Just clear your head!" He pulled his pipe from his mouth and pointed the stem at me. "Old Abercrombian saying: if given the opportunity, mini golf could save more lives than penicillin. Mental health, ya know?"

Finch muttered some choice words in retort of that nugget.

His great plan to get us out, get us distracted, and get us thinking had not quite worked. And so we'd gone through the motions at the Viking Mini-Golf for sixteen holes, most of them spent in silence–except for Gil's outbursts. We were almost done, and all I wanted to do was go back to the penthouse and get some sleep. A part of me believed that the new day would bring new luck and new possibility. Another part of me believed we couldn't be more ineffectual as a group.

I slapped the ball and watched it career away, knocking off the brick bumpers and ricochet towards the hole. The small red ball hit the viking's right boot and launched off the course, disappearing into a bush.

"I'm done," I said. "Sorry. I can't do it anymore."

"We'll find it!" Gil said. "Don't worry! Your ball is blue, so we know which one is yours."

"My ball is *red*, and I couldn't care less, Boss," I said. "I'm sorry, I just want to get out of here. I feel angry and helpless and sore and this is not helping."

"Me too," Willa said. She had not stopped frowning since our arrival.

"I'm *trying* to help," Gil said, lowering himself to all fours and sticking his arm into the small shrub. "This is maybe a little inappropriate, considering the missing kids..." he said, rummaging through a pile of brown leaves, "...but I think it's important. Not for the reasons you think I think it's important, but because we're still a team and we need some morale. We need some morale and we need clear heads, two things we do not have right now." He stopped, grunting as he dug his arm into the bush farther.

"You three are my family," he said. "And when times get tough, we're still together. We can't win all the cases, can't solve 'em all. Read my book and you'll see. Sometimes things just suck. Sometimes we lose. But this isn't over yet. Those kids are still out there, and we've got... what? four days to find them? You can do a lot in four days. I could build a whole Deep Space 9 out of Legos in that time." He sighed as his arm disappeared to the shoulder. "I love you guys and I don't like seein' you like this. We're together, damnit, and we're heroes, so stop actin' like we've already lost!"

He pulled his arm out—empty-handed—and cursed mightily. "Where is this damn ball?" he shouted. "You've got, like, *unlimited* magical power or whatever, man. Can't you find a *golf ball*?"

"What?"

"I said you've got—"

"That's a good idea," I said.

"What?"

"I can find Clarissa," I said.

"Dylan," Finch said, speaking for the first time since arriving at Viking Golf. "You aren't trained to locate a stranger. Do you know how difficult that is? I don't care for the word 'impossible,' but it is essentially—"

"But I'm not locating a total stranger, and it wouldn't be me looking," I said. "It would be the

214

vael."

"Semantics," Finch said. "You would still need to control–"

"No, Finch, you're forgetting something. Re-member when the vael connected Clarissa and I? When you two geniuses had me get a reading and–"

"Yes," Finch said, "I remember."

"Well, when that happened, she sort of left a fingerprint on my brain, same as I did on hers."

"And?"

"And with that I can find her," I said. "I don't know why, but I'm certain. We're connected. She left a trace on my brain." I closed my eyes and could feel it, as tangible as if I was touching her hand. I opened my eyes and smiled for the first time that day. We may not have been able to trust, well, *anyone*, but it was our first break.

"I can find her, guys," I said. "I know it. I can find her."

"It worked!" Gil shouted. "Mini golf saves the day! Again! Shazam, you cowpokes!"

CHAPTER 24. NO MAN'S LAND

Sometimes you get an idea and it *really* works.

This is rare for me, so let me savor it.

...

All right. Thanks.

It was dark, and Gil, Finch, and I stood outside a trailer in a small community called Long Neck. It had been about a fifteen or twenty minute drive outside of tourist central, and after a few long stretches of roads flanked by dense pine woods, here we were.

The vael had led us here.

What had begun as a crazy idea quickly mutated into a very real possibility. After leaving the Viking Golf place, I'd returned to my room in the penthouse and closed the door. With the lights out, I sat down on the bed and closed my eyes, doing everything I could to clear my mind and focus on what I was trying to do.

I didn't even need to try very hard.

If you've ever stared at a very bright light and then immediately closed your eyes–I'm sure this has happened–you see the ghostly image burned temporarily on your retina.

What I saw had been much brighter than that. It was like a fluorescent thread, floating in the otherwise empty expanse of my mind–yes, empty–leading me where I wanted to go. All I'd needed to do was hold onto that with minimal focus and it led us right... here.

Gil had a sword–freshly liberated from the Tank's trunk–while Finch had his trusty battle ax. Considering we didn't know what we were in for, I stuck with my .38. Standing in the dark front yard of the small, white trailer, I still didn't know what to expect. The yard was well kept. A stone birdbath stood in the center of the emerald green lawn. Beneath the trailer's front windows was a garden bed full of purple asters and yellow daisies. A short, red-hat-wearing stone garden gnome watched the scene unfold.

It was hard to imagine that inside the quaint dwelling, a Plague Doctor perhaps waited.

I was unable to get the skeleton face from my mind, complete with its wide, grinning mouth and gaping eye sockets.

"I'll go first," I whispered, walking up the narrow path to the front door. A short, wooden staircase led up to a screen door. The front door beyond it was closed, but through it I could hear laughter.

Gil, at my heels, caught me eye.

"Is that... laughing?" he whispered.

I nodded.

He shrugged.

I tried the screen door. It was unlocked. Slowly, I pulled it open, mindful of the inevitable *screeeeench* the door would make.

Wide open, I tried the doorknob. Locked.

"Hold the door," I whispered to Gil.

Silently, he held it wide. I stepped back, took a

deep breath, and leveled a kick at the door just between the knob and the deadbolt.

The frame cracked like a saltine and the door slammed open.

The television was on, and as I stepped into the room, gun raised, I heard screaming. I opened my mouth to mistakenly shout *POLICE!* (out of habit, really) when the lights flicked out.

Gil piled in behind me, swinging his sword wildly, Finch two steps behind him.

An orb of blue light lanced out of the darkness and struck Gil in the chest. One-armed as I was, I pointed my pistol, but blind in the blackness, held my fire. Gil was lifted off his feet and slammed into a bookshelf against the righthand wall.

"Gil!"

"Get out, you puppets!" a voice screeched to my left.

A second orb of blue light erupted from what looked like a kitchen, the ball of power aimed right at my head. I ducked as the circle ripped through the trailer's thin wall.

Beside me, Finch lowered his ax and launched a thin line of fire straight into the kitchen. In the flickering red light cast in its wake, I saw a number of women scatter.

"Urghghdrrr...." Gil muttered from the ground. I knelt at his side, pocketing my pistol, feeling in the darkness for blood. There wasn't any.

"Are you all right?"

"Get out, get out!" another voiced screamed in

the darkness.

An orb of light crashed through a window to my right, followed by a second that hit Finch at a glancing blow, spinning him around and throwing him to the floor.

"Clarissa?" I shouted. "Where are you?"

Suddenly, there was silence.

"Show yourself," a stern voice called.

Slowly, I stood.

"My name is–"

And one of those damned orbs slammed into my chest. I crumpled to the floor, unable to take a breath.

"Call the police!" a voice from the kitchen said, fear filling it. "Quick!"

"We can take care of them!" another said.

"W-w-wait," I gasped. "H-hold on."

"He's back on his feet," yet another voice said softly. "Myra, hit him again!"

"*NO!*" I said. "Please, wait. There's been a–"

One of the figures in the kitchen fired again, sending one of those balls of light straight at my face.

At the last second, Finch stepped in front of me, taking the impact full on. This time, he did not fall.

"Not so powerful when you lack surprise," he said softly.

"Who are you?" a voice called. "What is your name?"

"My name is Alistair Finch, and I mean you no harm."

"No harm?" an incredulous voice shouted. "You

219

kicked down my damned door!"

"For that, madame, I am truly sorry. I realize now that we have made a mistake. One of many, I must admit."

I took a tentative step forward. "What's going on?" I asked Finch softly.

"Well," he said, "we have found the coven."

***

Okay, so we hadn't found Clarissa. But technically, it was still a break.

After a few *really* awkward minutes, we all got calmed down and some kind lady decided to turn on the lights. Other than a softball-sized hole in the wall to the right of the front door and one smashed window, there wasn't much damage. Oh, and the broken front door, can't forget that.

"That kind of bullheaded entrance was totally unnecessary–"

"Really," Gil said, "We're very sorry."

"Who's going to fix–"

"I'll take care of it, I promise!"

"And the–"

"That too. Everything! Everything we busted!" Gil assured them. "I know a guy. A carpenter or whatever."

We were mostly squished onto a big U-shaped sectional sofa. Those who couldn't fit were either standing or seated on kitchen chairs pulled into the room, turning the U into a full circle.

The coven leader, a tall salt and pepper-haired woman with a fiercely angry face, had taken control of the conversation immediately.

"I imagine you will take care of everything," she said. "This is my sister's house and I won't have–"

"I apologize, Myra, I really do. We had no idea you were here."

"Who exactly did you expect to find?"

"Honestly? That black-robed thing," Gil said. "And Clarissa."

"You've seen the black figure?" a younger witch asked, leaning forward in her chair.

Gil nodded. "Unfortunately."

"How did you find us?" Myra asked. "We took great pains to stay hidden."

"Well, we found you by accident," Gil said. "You ladies aren't the only ones with powers, and the big guy there found you using a little power of his own."

Myra turned an impressed eye in my direction. "You practice?" she asked.

"A little," I said.

"He's a modest guy!" Gil said. "He's got enough power to knock the moon out of orbit!"

"Doubtful," Myra said. "But still, *how* did you find us?"

"I was looking for Clarissa," I said. "She and I... well, accidentally connected once. We had a connection, so I thought that if I tried to use that to find her, it would work." I shrugged. "Obviously, I was wrong."

"Maybe not," Myra said. "We were... to be honest with you, we were trying to find Clarissa, as well."

"You were?" I asked. "How?"

Myra leaned over and spoke softly to a younger woman beside her. The younger woman nodded and stood up. Moving quickly, she slipped through the crowded room and raced down a hallway to the back.

We sat in silence, waiting.

"So..." Gil said, after a long moment. "All you ladies are staying here? And you have been for a while?"

A few nodded.

"That's a lotta ladies in a small space," he said.

No response.

"You all use that one bathroom?"

Definitely no response.

A *thump* of feet heralded the return of the younger witch from the back. In her hand, she carried a small wooden box. She handed it to Myra.

"We were doing a spell, you see." She opened the box, revealing a small tied bundle of hair.

"Is that Clarissa's?" I asked. "Where did you get—"

"From her apartment," Myra said. "You'd be surprised how much hair you can retrieve from a hairbrush."

"So it was you," Gil said, pointing. "*You* wrecked her place looking for hair!?"

"What? No!" Myra asked, genuinely confused.

"Uh, okay," Gil said, backtracking. "Maybe not."

"We went over there in the early morning hours, looking for Clarissa. We've had enough of her involvement in this and we decided to do something to put a stop to it! Margaret was performing a tracking spell when you–"

"That's it!" Gil said. "The streams got crossed. Your search and their search got knotted! You should never cross the streams!" he shouted, making an *X* with two fingers. "Haven't you guys seen *Ghost-busters*? Anybody? Oh, come on!"

"All right, Boss, all right," I turned back to Myra. "What do you mean her 'involvement'?" I asked. "How was Clarissa involved?"

"If you are as innocent as you would have us believe," Myra said, "then you must know she is involved in these kidnappings."

"What makes you say that?"

"Clarissa has been a friend to that entire department," Myra said. "She has been associating with all of them, and they are clearly evil. They've done nothing to stop these kidnappings, spent far too much time searching for *us*, bullied witnesses–"

"Hold on, searching for you?" I asked. "What do you mean?"

"That Sheriff Huggins," Myra said, "don't trust him. He gets that Deputy of his to do his dirty work. What's his name... Donnelly. The one who shot you!"

"That's right, we read all about it in the papers!" a stocky witch with black hair chimed in.

"That we did," Myra added. "Huggins has done nothing but send his attack dog out to–"

"Hold on," I interrupted. "I'm sorry, but what do you mean attack dog? What's he done?"

"He's been after us!" Myra said, shaking her head. "Huggins wants us bad for those kidnappings, but we've got nothing to do with them!"

My mind started turning, the rusty gears in my brain finally deciding to *do* something.

"Plus," Myra continued, "we've seen that Deputy Donnelly bully witnesses like there was no tomorrow!"

"What do you mean 'bully witnesses'?" I asked. "Start at the top."

"All right, all right," Myra said. "We've been involved with this case since the first kidnapping, the young boy at the hotel? We cast runes at the hotel, searching for guidance. We did it again at Fort Miles–"

"It was *you* who cast the runes?" Gil asked.

"Of course it was! When things didn't pan out, we started to watch the police. We put *them* under surveillance, just like they did us. We knew something funny was happening when nothing came of our runes *or* our spells."

"You watched the police?"

"That's right. We drew lots, and Agatha got that pit bull deputy."

"I sure did," a slight redhead added. "He's trouble, he is."

"What did you see?"

"He was talking to our neighbors and staking out our houses," Myra said, speaking for the younger witch. "He watched our jobs and watched our friends' houses. We've had to keep on the move since this started. That Sheriff Huggins has been after us. He thinks we took those kids!"

"No," I said, almost to myself. "Huggins doesn't buy into magic. He doesn't think it's you. You're not even on his radar–"

"Then Agatha sees the deputy bullying that hotel owner out on Route 1. How many times did he go to see him, Agatha?"

"Six or seven," Agatha said, nodding.

"That's right, six or seven. And each time the cop dragged him into a room, shouting and carrying on."

"Well, he was a suspect, wasn't he?" Gil asked.

"That's no way to treat a suspect!" Myra said. "Innocent until proven guilty in this country, right?"

"Well, yeah, I think you've got a good point there, Myra."

"I know I do! So anyway, that Deputy Donnelly has been bullying witnesses–"

"Wait," I said. "Stop."

"What? What's wrong?"

"How many times did that deputy go to the hotel to talk to Raleigh?"

"Raleigh?"

"That's the hotel owner."

"Oh, Agatha said six or seven."

"Six or seven?" I asked, my mind racing. When I'd been at the hotel, chasing Jane, I remember seeing the Rehoboth Police Department cruiser in the lot. But things were beginning to come together, and slowly–very slowly–I could see that they weren't adding up. The puzzle pieces I was just getting weren't *quite* fitting in with the pieces I'd been col-lecting.

"That's it!" I said, interrupting Myra mid-rant.

"What? What's it?" she asked.

"Deputy Donnelly," I said. "And Fred Raleigh, the hotel guy. That's it."

"What? Why? Are you loopy, son?"

"The Ocean Hotel is in Lewes," I said. "It's outside of Rehoboth jurisdiction. There was no reason for Deputy Donnelly *ever* to question Fred Raleigh."

"Unless–"

"He wasn't questioning him," I said. "He was going to talk to him. Talk to him about *this*. That's why Donnelly was looking for you, not because of the Sheriff, but because he knew you were investigating the disappearances. It's not Clarissa, and it's not the Sheriff, it's the Deputy and the hotel guy, Raleigh. They're in this together. And we've got to find them." I looked up at the room of faces looking at me.

"We find them, we find the kids."

CHAPTER 25. CRYIN' SHAME

We left the witches' humble abode sometime before dawn. At a certain point, the tables turned and they started to squeeze *us* for information. By the time we left, we were pretty spent.

Driving the Tank through the deserted streets, I called Willa, holding the phone with my bad arm.

"Any headway?" I asked.

"Not much. I'm trying to get ahold of someone at the USGS to–"

"The what?"

"The US Geological Survey. I'm trying to get ahold of someone at the USGS to try and get some kind of map of these telluric currents. The problem is no one's there."

"It's 5:30 in the morning, Will'," I said. "They'll get there eventually."

"We don't have much time to waste," Willa said.

"Well, we don't, but if they're not there, then... they're not there."

"What did you guys find? Did you find Clarissa? Judging by your interest in the USGS, I'm guessing not."

"No," I said. I gave her a brief rundown on the

coven and what we learned. "So we may not have found Clarissa, but we're definitely pointed in the right direction."

"So I should look for this Deputy now?"

"Yeah, Donnelly. What was his real name? Leachman?"

"William, yeah." She took a deep breath and sighed. "All right, I'm on it."

"And don't forget the FBI guy who got him outta hock. Special Agent Allagash. Right now, we're gonna head to the Ocean Hotel first, try and get a bead on this Raleigh guy. He should be easier to find. Just raise your antennas on Donnelly or Leachman or whatever, and try to get a fix on these telluric currents. I'll be in touch."

We said our goodbyes and hung up.

"Anything?" Gil asked.

I shook my head. "Still in a holding pattern."

"Then let's get this Raleigh guy," Gil said, cracking his knuckles. "I bet Finch has some primo questions he'd like to ask."

***

The Ocean Hotel was just as boring and non-descript as I remembered it. At this hour, the park-ing lot was filled, so I parked the Tank in the back by the laundry room. The sun was up, but nearly all the lights in each row of rooms was dark, but the only light I cared about was lit, and from a distance I could see a silhouette moving around in the manager's office.

I was very cognizant of my pistol, holstered on my belt in the small of my back. I pulled my shirt lower, making sure it was covered. I could feel adrenaline start to pump in anticipation.

With Gil and Finch behind me, I pushed open the door and stepped into the hot office.

"Good mornin'! What can I do for you, stranger!"

"Where's Raleigh?" I asked.

A young man with curly brown hair was behind the desk, sweating and reading *Guns & Ammo*.

"Mr. Raleigh? As a matter of fact, he's on vacation. His first day off was yesterday."

I remembered his words about never taking a day off since he bought the place. "Any idea when he'll be back?"

"Yup," he pulled an agenda book from beneath the desk and flipped it open and pointed at a day. "He'll be back next Sunday."

"Let me see that." I grabbed the book and turned it around to face me.

"Hey now, you can't–"

"Relax kid," Gil said, slapping a $100 bill on the counter. "Why not get some fresh air?"

"What? Do you want me to step out or something?" he asked, pocketing the bill.

"You're pretty sharp, slugger," Gil said, smiling. "So yeah, beat it and let us get curious for a minute, eh?"

"You got it. I'm not paid enough to ignore a hundred bucks." He stood and walked out, whistling.

Finch rounded the desk and began rummaging

through the paperwork. Most of it was legit hotel receipts and registration forms.

The planner was not as helpful as I'd hoped. The days were marked with various names and numbers beside them; I assumed they were reservations.

Unfortunately, there were no big red **X**s marking dates of multiple human sacrifices–typical for hotel reservation books, I suppose, but disappointing none-theless.

"Look at this," Finch said, pulling out a second agenda. He flipped the book open to July and pointed.

"A big red X!" Gil said. "Holy Harvey Birdman, that is amazing!" He looked at me. "I guess you don't find those much in any hotel reservation books, eh?"

"I was just thinking that," I said, smiling.

"I am sorry to interrupt, but look at the day," Finch said.

"The day?" I said.

"That's..." Gil squinted.

"That's today," I said.

"What about the quarter phaser whatever–" Gil sputtered.

I shook my head. "Between moon phases and big red Xs, I'll take the big red X."

"What now?" Gil asked. "Is Willa–"

My phone rang in my pocket. "That's probably her now," I said. "She's trying to get a fix on Donnelly and some kind of map of these telluric line things." I opened my old flip phone and said, "Willa, what's–"

"This is Sheriff Huggins, Mr. Dylan, I'm sorry to call so early–"

"That's all right," I said, speaking slowly, cautiously. My last run in with the good Sheriff Huggins had been rather interesting, as you can remember. He sounded just as tentative as I felt. "What can I do for you Sheriff?"

"I'm... well, I'm tryin' to make up for my bullheadedness," he said. "My pride. There's been a development this morning, and I thought you should know about it. So, I'm calling."

I could tell it was hard for the Sheriff to say any of this, so I decided not to rub anything in, even if I could have. No 'I told you so' was necessary.

"I very much appreciate that," I said honestly. "What happened?"

"It's better for you to see, I think. Do you know where the Charles Cullen Bridge is? The one that'll take you south of Dewey? To Bethany and Fenwick?"

Point of fact, I did.

***

South of Rehoboth lies Dewey, a college kids' party town. If you keep driving south, you get to a long stretch of empty road as Route 1 passes through the ten or so miles of Delaware Seashore State Park leading to the Indian River Inlet. Crossing the Indian River Inlet and taking you to Bethany and points south, is the trusty Charles Cullen Bridge. When I pulled off the road at the base of it, I almost didn't recognize it.

"They've been working on this," I said. "It didn't

look like this when I was a kid."

"What are we doing here?" Finch asked sourly.

"I don't know, honestly, but the Sheriff thought we should see something, so let's see it." I pointed at a pair of flashing lights atop a police cruiser parked on the north shore beneath the bridge. Together, Gil, Finch, and I walked over the dunes towards the lights.

The Sheriff was there, standing on the rocky shoreline, talking to another officer I didn't recognize. When Huggins saw us approaching, he said something to the other officer, excusing himself.

"Sheriff," I said.

"Good morning. You made good time."

"We were... running errands."

If he took pause to three grown men "running errands" at 6AM, he didn't show it. "That there's the Bethany Sheriff," he said, nodding at the other officer. "He's got jurisdiction here, but he's doing me a favor."

"What's this about?"

"Come here," he said.

Overhead, cards whipped over the bridge seams, a double *thump thump* for each pair of tires that rumbled over them. Down by the water, the wind picked up in a salty spray.

I tried to ignore the van from the medical examiner on my left. It was harder to ignore the body that lay covered on the sand.

My stomach swirled as the Sheriff knelt beside the body and pulled back the sheet.

"Oh," I said.

"Oh?"

"I was... well, I was a little... spooked that it might be somebody else," I admitted.

"Clarissa?"

I nodded. "Yeah."

Deputy Donnelly stared up at me with dead eyes.

"I wasn't expecting him," I said. Behind me, Gil turned away. He was not good with these things.

Finch knelt across the body from Huggins. "Do you have a pair of gloves, Sheriff?" he asked.

Dubiously, the Sheriff pulled a pair of rubber gloves from his breast pocket and handed them over. "Now don't go–"

"I'll be careful," Finch said.

Huggins looked up at me, doubt evident in his eyes, and I could tell he regretted calling us already–to say nothing of giving Finch the gloves.

I met his gaze. "Aren't you going to ask me?"

"What?"

"Where I was last night?"

Huggins took a breath and held it.

"I was with these two," I said. "We played mini golf and then–"

He shook his head. "Thankfully, I don't need to know."

"What do you mean?"

"It's outta my jurisdiction," he said. "Plus, this guy was with that FBI agent. So I'd say you are no longer the number one suspect."

"That's true," I said. Did Allagash do this? If so, why? Until that moment, I'd assumed they were working together.

"He has been beaten," Finch said, lowering the sheet further. "And perhaps tortured."

"The M.E. thinks that the wounds on the body are from the rocks," Huggins said. "The body was in the drink when we got the call, and the rocks here are like daggers."

"Some of these wounds were caused by the rocks," Finch said, "but not all of them." He pulled down the man's tee at the neck and pointed out welts and bruising along his collarbone. "Bruising is pre-mortem," he said. "And his shirt has extensive blood-stains on it."

"Couldn't that have been caused by–"

"This was not a boating accident, Sheriff," Gil said.

"This should convince you," Finch said, sighing. He pried open Donnelly's jaws.

A number of teeth were missing, ragged bloody holes in their place.

Huggins withdrew, turning his head in disgust. "What did that?"

"A man," Finch said. "A man pulled these teeth out. As I said, he was tortured."

CHAPTER 26. THE WAY

I told the Sheriff that Raleigh was his man. He asked me a few pointed questions about where, why, and how. When he was finished, I drove us back to the penthouse.

"Why'd you tell him we're looking for this Raleigh guy?" Gil asked.

I shrugged. "A fair trade. He didn't need to call us in on this, but he did."

"He probably figured out that we're not as bad as he thought," Gil muttered. "If he'd called us earlier–"

"I know," I interrupted. I couldn't bear to run through the same old argument again. I'd done it enough times in my head. "I don't think he'll find him, but we need all the help we can get."

Finch unlocked the front door. Willa was pacing, on the phone.

"I understand that, Doctor," she said, her voice riddled with annoyance. "I just need you to send me your best–" she stopped, listening. "*No*," she said. "I need whatever you have that's most up to date... *yes*, exactly. You'll send it now? Thank you." She disconnected and looked up at us. "That was grueling," she said.

"What happened?"

"A simple question turned into a lecture." She frowned. "What's wrong?"

"Donnelly is dead," Gil said.

"So I guess I can call off the search?"

I nodded. "Call it off, and ramp up the search on Raleigh and this Allagash agent."

"Raleigh is missing, too?"

"Yeah," Gil said. "And we don't have any time left."

"What do you mean?"

I explained the part about the big **X** and Willa just shook her head. "How can we find an FBI agent and some hotel nutjob in twelve hours?"

"Suddenly a needle in a haystack doesn't sound so bad, does it?" Finch asked, taking a seat.

"No, it doesn't."

Willa sat at her computer, head down. "Looks like Huggins has an APB out on Raleigh already."

"Good man," I said. "He could get lucky."

"He could," she said. "If we knew anything about this Allagash, that would help, too."

"We don't, do we?"

She shook her head. "I've got a call out to a guy at the bureau that I worked with once, but it's been a while. I'm not very optimistic. It was a long shot anyway."

"You've worked with a guy at the bureau?" Gil asked. "What do you do again?"

She smiled. "I... locate information. Don't worry about it."

"Whatever."

"Anyway, I'm hoping he gets back to me. But it's been almost three days."

"What about this USGS thing?" I asked.

She clicked something on her computer and waited. "It's coming in now," she said. *Click. Click click.*

"Okay, I don't know what I was expecting, but it wasn't this."

Gil, Finch, and I walked over.

On the screen was a satellite image of the world in a Mercator projection. Sweeping across the map were a number of swirls and circles reminiscent of a great fingerprint, the largest hovering over South America, the Pacific Ocean, and the Atlantic Ocean/Eastern Seaboard.

"Are those the telluric currents?" I asked.

Willa nodded. "And it looks like one sweeps across the coast right about..." she pointed. "*Here.*"

"Where's that?" Gil asked, tapping the screen.

She batted his hand away. "It's an island," Willa said, zooming in to the large satellite image. "Burton Island," she read. "It's part of a nature preserve. South of here."

"I know where it is," I said.

"Looks like it's uninhabited," Willa continued. "From the map, most of it looks like marshes and wetlands. And there are a lot of woods too. Dense, evergreen woods."

"How big is it?" I asked.

"Not too big," Willa said, "but it's big enough. If

237

we go, we'll need to to sneak in. The island is only open on Sundays."

"*Only open on Sundays*?" Gil asked. "What is it, a friggin' *Chick-Fil-A*? Or... the anti-*Chick-Fil-A*? Does that make sense?"

"They're afraid of hikers being on the island while hunters are nearby–"

"So yeah, we need to sneak on," I said.

"I got an idea," Gil said. "Finch, where's your phone?"

"Why?"

"We're not going in the front way. I'm not a fan of sneaking past park rangers considering this isn't *Scooby Doo*."

"What do you mean, Boss?" Finch asked.

"I'm gonna charter a boat! I like boats!"

Willa pointed at the map. "That's a good idea. The whole backside of the island sits open in the Indian River Bay. We could rent a boat in Dewey and shoot straight down. It's not far."

"We'll still need help," I said. "We're running out of time, and we'll need to cover this whole island."

"We could call the Sheriff–" Gil began.

"No," I said. "I think we all agree he's probably trustworthy–"

"Well, yeah," Gil said.

"–but I still don't think he should get involved with this. We don't know this Raleigh guy, and we don't know what the Plague Doctor is capable of doing."

"So who do we call?" Willa asked.

I looked up at her. "Well, I could call..."

"No," she said. "She wouldn't even help if you asked!"

I smiled. "Let's find out," I said.

I stepped out on the porch to call Jane. I figured alone was better. A little less awkward.

She answered on the first ring.

"Hey Jane, it's me. Um, Dylan. Listen, I'm sorry to call, but I need your–"

"I've been listening," she said. "What time do we leave?"

***

All right, so it was creepy, but given the circumstances, I didn't ask any questions. That would be for later.

When I came back in, all I did was nod.

"No way," Willa said. "No way would she–"

"Why is it so hard to believe that she–"

"She's a *thief*, Dylan," Willa said. "She shouldn't be trusted. She can't be!"

"There are worse people than thieves," Finch said.

"You're supposed to be on my side, Finch," Willa said.

Finch shrugged. "Am I mistaken in pointing out your less-than-wholesome methods of acquiring bank account information in this very story? Besides, we need help. I don't care much *who* it is."

"Gil?" Willa said with a groan, turning to him for support.

"What? She's not so bad. I wouldn't do what *he* did with her," he said, pointing at me and mock shivering. "And yeah, Finch explained it to me. That is gross. But like the old man said, there are worse things than thieves."

Willa sighed. "I just don't like it. I don't trust–"

Her phone rang.

"Oh," she said, answering it quickly. "Hello? Yes, hello Mark, how are you? Oh, good, you know, same old. Thank you for getting back to me, I know you must be busy–"

She slipped past me, walking out onto the balcony I'd just vacated.

"Mark?" I asked the room.

Gil shrugged.

When she came back inside, she was frowning. "That was Mark Robson," she said. "He's my FBI guy."

"What'd he say about Allagash?"

"Well he said that a Bureau-wide memo went out on Allagash. He's missing, basically presumed AWOL. There's a warrant out for his arrest."

"Does Mark know Allagash?"

She nodded. "They've met once or twice. Mark said... well, he said that if Allagash is involved, it's bad."

"Why?"

"Allagash is former special forces. Black ops, recruited straight from the military. Mark said that if Allagash is here... then we're in trouble. The FBI can dispatch a field team, but it would be at least twenty-four hours before their arrival."

"What? Twenty-four hours? That's too late," I said, shaking my head.

She nodded. "Yeah. The local unit is following a lead in Salisbury right now. So it looks like we're on our own."

"Good," Gil said. "We got this."

I almost smiled. *Almost*. His endless resiliency and confidence were admirable, and they usually went a long way in reassuring me. Today, however, they didn't help calm my nerves one iota, and looking at Willa, I could tell I wasn't alone. The Zeros vs. Rogue Black Ops FBI Agent + Crazy Hotel Owner + Undead Reanimated Skeleton Medieval Plague Doctor? And what were the stakes again? Oh, just the human sacrifice of three innocent children and probably our new witch friend Clarissa? Fantastic!

I looked at Gil. His smile was unwavering.

"Suit up," he said.

CHAPTER 27. GIVE IT ALL UP

By the time the five of us got onto the water, it was midday. Willa made some sandwiches that we ate on our rented boat. I drove, because I was the only one who knew how, grateful that the sound of the sloop's outboard engine removed small talk from the equation.

The drive to the Dewey marina had been awkward. As usual, I drove and Gil sat shotgun. That left Finch, Willa, and Jane to share the back seat. Finch had volunteered for the middle, wisely separating Willa and Jane. Any other guy would have felt uncomfortable back there, but thankfully Finch was emotionally removed enough not to mind–or not to care.

And so here we were, eating tuna sandwiches as the small sloop cut through the bay's pungent water. Jane was back in her black catsuit, business as usual. Gil had donned a black Hawaiian shirt with yellow sugar skulls, Bermuda shorts, and his trusty deerstalker hat, his unlit pipe clamped between his teeth. Willa wore a black tank-top with jeans that tucked into newly purchased hiking boots. Finch was dressed all in black–no surprise there. I wore jeans and a white tee shirt. No one was talking. The only high-light of the ride turned out to be Gil getting sick over the side.

The Rehoboth Bay narrowed at a place called–no joke–Raccoon Cove, beyond which lay a sandbar the map marked Hawkins Point, heralding the small island of Burton Island, marking the entrance to Indian River Bay. I throttled down on the engines, slowing the sloop down to only a few knots.

"Where do you want to go?" Gil asked. "That way? Or that way?"

The Indian River Bay was crowded with sailors and fishermen, with our current drifting location proving to be the least populated spot in sight.

"If we cut inland," I said, pointing to my left, "we may be able to..."

Willa stumbled against the current, raising the map and moving towards me. "That's the island there, isn't it?" she said, pointing straight ahead.

I nodded. "I kinda figured we'd move around to the southwest side and try to dock there."

"You will be exposed to the bay on that side," Jane said, walking over and handling the rocking of the waves much better than either of us. Willa gave her a look. A bad look.

Jane continued, "You could go to shore–"

"–here," Willa interrupted, pointed.

Jane paused, glancing at the other woman. "Yes, there," she agreed, pointing to the same spot.

"What does that say?" Gil said, lurching towards us, squinting, handling the ship's rocking worse than any of us.

"Sawpit Cove," I read. "What a name."

"It's marshy, so there shouldn't be a lot of boaters

drawing up on the beaches," Willa said. "There aren't any beaches at all, actually."

"And there are a few other empty islands to the northeast, offering plenty of cover."

Willa nodded. "And the yacht moorings in this inlet here," she pointed, "this... this Balders Pond, will be obscured by the east side of Burton Island."

"It's perfect," I said.

"Yes," Willa said, "I think it is."

I looked up at Gil, looking a little green, and Finch, looking a little bored.

"Get ready to dock, guys. Next stop, Sawpit Cove."

***

The cove itself was little more than a tiny harbor surrounded by swamp. I throttled the boat up onto a mudflat and cut the engine. Off to my right, a hopping jet ski shot past, bouncing up and down on the bay's tide.

"Let's go," I said, pulling the key from the ignition.

Gil opened the bench storage unit that we'd filled with goodies from the Tank's trunk. He started passing out weapons. Finch took a sword. Gil a double-sided ax. I slipped my short sword's sheath across my chest like a bandolier–I still had my .38 in my belt, too. Jane took a pair of long knives, belting them around her slim waist. Willa just took a Maglite flashlight.

"Weapons..." she said, glancing uncomfortably at

Jane, "...aren't really my thing."

"Okay ladies and gents," Gil said finally. "Time to go. You wanna go first, big man?" He peered over the gunwale, eyes wide.

Beside him, Jane was frowning in her black catsuit, arms crossed over her chest.

"What?" I asked.

"I was hoping not to have to climb through two hundred yards of mud."

Willa smirked as she tied her boots tighter. "Should have dressed for the occasion," she said.

"Uh, why did you wear that?" I asked Jane.

"These are my work clothes, all right?"

"It's day," I continued. "You actually stick out *more* in that—"

"Yes, I know," she grumbled. "I realized that at the damned water park the day you—"

"—yeah, right? You really stuck out there—"

"Are you two ready?" Willa interrupted.

"Uh, yeah."

Turns out Willa was the first over the side, sinking over the ankle in the mud. As she *squelched* into the marshy ground, a putrid methane rush of air bubbled up at us.

"Marsh gas," Gil frowned. "I... yeah, I sorta forgot about that." He shook his head like a small child. "Smells like farts."

"It's not... so bad," Willa said, breathing through her mouth.

Finch followed, leaping the gunwale and

splashing down beside Willa. Slowly, they began trudging towards more solid land. Jane jumped next. I followed.

Gil was last, muttering curses the whole way. His big white sneakers were the worst suited for the deep mud.

The only thing worse than the mud and brown water that soaked through everything was the swarm of bugs that seemed to rise off the marsh the farther inland we got.

Mosquitos and black flies moved around us in a huge cloud. I put my head down and surged forward. Gil, the caboose, squawked and hollered the whole way.

When I finally stepped onto dry ground, I was exhausted and bitten to hell.

"This is... fun," I muttered. It was mid-afternoon already, and the sun was beginning to move down in the western sky. From where we stood at the mouth of the pine woods, catching our breath, the dense forest was surprisingly dark.

"The woods start here," Willa said, "and continue south before growing. There's a pond in the middle of the island, and the forest fills out around it."

"There's a lotta woods," Gil said, slapping at a bug on his neck.

"There's enough," Willa said. "The biggest stretch is on the backside of the pond, running from the pond to the Bay. Farther to the east," she pointed, "there's another dense patch of woods. The hiking trail cuts through that bit. The whole island is less than half a mile long," she said. "But it's... well, it's dense.

And it'll be slow going. This whole part is untouched. No trails, no nothing."

Gil spun a black nylon bag off his shoulder. "Walkies!" he said, pulling our trusty plastic walkie talkies out of the bag. "Hand 'em out. And check your batteries!"

The five of us each grabbed one and flicked it on. Gil demanded that we spread, out moving far enough away from each other to make sure the walkies worked. They did.

"Okay," Gil said. "Try and stay off the channels, save your batteries. We don't know how long this could take. Our call signs will be–"

"We're just going to use our names," Willa said.

"What? Why can't we use the call signs?" Gil sighed.

"Let's keep it simple," Willa said.

"*You* keep it simple," Gil smiled. "I'm stickin' with call signs. I like that. Big Papa," he said pointing at me; "Cat Woman," pointing at Jane; "Fogey," pointing at Finch; "and Angry Hacker," he said, pointing at Willa. "Oh, and call me El Jefe."

"Whatever," Willa said.

"So call if you see anything suspicious," I said. "Keep your eyes on the ground for footprints or markings of any kind. It should be pretty easy to spot anything manmade here. There shouldn't *be* anything manmade, so if there is, it's probably from Raleigh or Allagash."

Gil cleared his throat. "Did you, uh, try to use that locating thing on Clarissa again? I know last time we just found the coven, but if she's nearby..."

"I tried," I admitted. "I... I couldn't feel her at all." I didn't say what I was thinking, what I was *dreading*. If I couldn't feel her presence, that meant that she was either very, *very* far away, or that she was...

Dead?

I shook the thought off. "Let's go," I said. "Split up."

"Teams of two?" Gil suggested.

I shook my head. "Too much area to cover. Too little time." I looked at our gang of Zeros. "So we split up."

"Good luck, gang," Gil said. "We'll be all right; the kids will be all right."

No one said anything, and no one moved.

"You heard the man," I said. "Let's get lost."

***

Before splitting up, Willa showed us the map, pointing to our current location at the northwest corner of the island. The forest sliced across the marshes, moving southeast, before blooming at the center of the island. Beyond the forest lay the pond. Just beyond the pond, the forest grew to fill the full width of the island. Somewhere in that tangled mess, three innocent children awaited their doom along with a probably-kidnapped psychic witch named Clarissa.

I didn't even want to think about the possibility that we were wrong. It wasn't out of the question that we were the only people on the island.

I buried that thought and started into the forest. The other Zeros followed, fanning out behind me, weapons drawn.

Five minutes later, I heard nothing but the sound of the bay and the rustle of the wind in the trees. My companions may as well have been on the moon. In the dense foliage, I couldn't see more than five or ten feet in any direction. Each step was difficult, forcing me to push through tangled branches and climb over downed trees. The ground was mostly solid, although every now and then I stepped down and felt my foot slip into marshy water. The swamp was never far away.

I made slow progress, the sun seeming to mock me as it sank in the sky. I tried to move faster, but each step was a battle. Before I knew it, twilight had descended in a red and purple cascade.

I was winded, and I could feel cuts on my face and arms from sharp branches and thorn bushes that surrounded me. Taking a breather, I sat on a fallen tree trunk and pulled out my walkie.

"Anybody got anything?" I asked, breathing heavily.

One by one, the Zeros sounded off, each sounding as tired as I did.

The resounding answer was, "No," except from Gil, who said, "*Negatory, Big Papa.*"

I raised the walkie to my mouth, ready to give some encouragement, offer some on-the-fly audible that could be the game-changer we needed.

But there was nothing. I was completely bereft of ideas.

I lowered the walkie and saw the red **LOW BAT** light had illuminated. "Great," I sighed.

Above me, the sun sank further.

***

Night had fallen.

The deeper into the woods I'd gotten, the darker it had become. When night had fallen in earnest, I realized how foolish I'd been not to bring a light. My left arm was in a sling, still bandaged heavily from where the late Deputy Donnelly had shot me, and with one arm incapacitated, I was in a tight spot. The walkie was clipped to my belt, and in my right hand I carried the .38. I couldn't direct any vael-powered light with my bad arm, not in a sling, at least.

At some point, I pulled the sling gingerly off, carefully releasing my arm. The pain was still there, but infinitely less than it had been. Cautiously, I pushed a little power through my left arm, afraid the energy would bust open my stitches.

It didn't, and a soft white light filled the cramped space I'd carved out in the woods.

Above me, a canopy of branches completely cut me off from the outside world, and I felt like I was trapped in a cage. Half of me wanted to turn back, certain at this point that this was a mistake. Clarissa and the kids were somewhere else, I thought, about to be killed by a madman while my friends and I stumbled around, lost in the woods.

But with no other recourse, I did the only thing I could: I pushed on.

A few minutes later, I stopped. Somewhere in the darkness to my left, I heard the sound of leaves being crushed underfoot.

I extinguished the light coming from my bad side and waited, certain I'd imagined it.

I heard it again, the faint *crinkle* of leaves and *snap* of a twig.

Tentatively, I took a step in that direction, my boot inching along the soft soil. One step followed the first, and soon I had halved the distance between myself and the other sound.

Closing my eyes, I reached out, looking for some kind of magical signature. If it was Gil or Finch, I'd be able to tell; I'd be able to *feel* the command they had over otherworld power.

I felt nothing.

A thicker branch *cracked*, and I froze, holding my breath. Slowly, I cocked the .38 and raised it.

A flutter of motion erupted from the darkness ahead of me, and I ducked unconsciously. Another branch broke. I jumped forward, vaulting a tree limb. Somewhere to my right, I heard a voice shout something unintelligible.

I raised my gun into the air and fired it. "Don't move!" I shouted, sending a pulse of light shooting forward from my left hand.

Ahead of me, a long-limbed bird stared, wide-eyed.

"What the fu–"

Something slammed into me from my right, and my pistol fired again. I fell onto my right side and hollered in pain as my stitches ripped open. Wings flapped as the bird lifted off. Light still poured from my left hand, but the light seemed buried beneath a blanket, extinguished. I jammed my right elbow back, connecting solidly with something.

"You are *not* the kind of doctor I need," I said through gritted teeth as I turned to face the Plague Doctor pinning me down.

Its mask was gone, and two gaping black eye sockets peered back at me as one bony hand closed around my throat. Slowly, the mouth opened. I fought back, muscles tensing, firing the gun and sending a bullet ineffectually into the ground.

The Plague Doctor's jaw began to clack, *open close*, *open close*, *open close*, repeatedly. It picked up speed until I heard that same sound I'd heard that night on the bluff at Fort Miles. A *clack clack clack clack clack clack* of teeth.

The bony fingers tightened on my throat. I opened my mouth to breath and couldn't even gasp. My airway was closed. The Plague Doctor's second hand closed on my right wrist, unnatural strength turning my gunhand towards me. Long bone fingers slith-ered to the trigger, grasp tightening.

Blood was pooling in my open left hand, but gritting my teeth, I turned, raising my bad arm and turning it back towards the Plague Doctor as my vision began to dim. I needed air, and I needed it *immediately*. I closed my left hand on the creature's skull, squeezing and pulling, hoping to use torque and spin the skeleton off me. Nothing worked.

The barrel of my pistol crept closer to my heart as my vision darkened further.

Unconsciousness wasn't far away now.

The vael seemed to rip my chest apart, sending a lightning bolt of energy through my entire body. My left hand closed like a vise on the skull, cracking the bone.

The *clack clack clack clack* of teeth stopped. The skeleton opened its mouth wide and wailed, a low plaintive sound escaping its jaws.

I squeezed tighter, the power of the vael filling me with unnatural power.

In my hand, the skull imploded, crushed to powder and bony fragments.

Still, the mouth hung open, wailing.

I took a jagged breath, the hand on my throat now limp, and pushed the skeleton off me. I kicked it away and skittered back.

It continued to moan.

"*H-h-heeelp,*" I gasped, my voice barely a whisper.

I reached for my walkie, but it was gone, knocked loose during the struggled.

To my right, maybe fifty yards out, I heard a voice shouting.

It was Gil.

I stumbled to my feet and began lurching towards his voice, branches slapping at my face as I pushed light out from my left hand. The .38 was locked in my right hand in a death grip.

Around me, the forest was coming to life, rustling of branches and the snapping of twigs was filling the once quiet woods. Footfalls sounded to my left and right, but I ignored them. I had to get to Gil.

Finally, I burst through a thick bush and collapsed in a small opening, a fire burning in its center. Rising to my knees, I saw Gil standing over a bloody and unconscious Willa, swiping his ax at the foreboding shape of a Plague Doctor, the ax ripping through black robes and revealing bones beneath. In the flickering orange light, I could see Gil had blood smeared across his face, but it didn't slow him one bit.

To my left, a second Plague Doctor ripped from the cover of trees and threw its body on the fire, the flames devouring his robe at first before flickering and dimming. The creature was smothering the fire.

"No," I said, pocketing the pistol in exchange for my short sword. The last thing we needed was darkness. "Get off!" I shouted, swinging the blade down *cracking* straight through its spinal column, ending its flailing motions. I called power into my fist and launched a column of fire into the creature's back, engulfing it in flame.

The clearing lit up. Jane burst from the woods to my right with Finch at her side. I turned to them, and opened my mouth to give instructions when *three* more Plague Doctors exploded from the forest, long-nosed masked faces buried in flowing black robes. Bony arms closed around Jane and Finch as the two drew their weapons and turned to fight.

I took a step towards my friends and stopped,

remembering Finch's words: "Someone must control them," he'd said. These creatures didn't act alone.

Against my better judgement, I turned my back on Finch and Jane, Gil and Willa, and I ran into the woods on the other side of the clearing.

Eyes closed, I reached out, the power of the vael still churning heavily in me. I imagined Clarissa, I grasped at the thread that was her being. I felt the mark she'd left on me and used it to hone in on her. She was close, I knew it, she had to be. Still, I felt nothing.

I crashed through the branches and tripped, falling facedown in a muddy recess in the ground. As I stumbled to my feet, I froze.

A voice spoke, somewhere ahead of me. Somehow, over the din of the roaring flame and shouting behind me, it was unmistakable.

I ran towards it, sword at the ready.

The woods ended, and I was on the beach. A bonfire raged, flames shooting at least ten feet into the air. Fred Raleigh, Ocean Hotel owner and manager, knelt before the conflagration, arms raised and reciting some spell in Latin.

On the other side of the fire, I saw the gagged and bound shapes of the three children and Clarissa.

Raleigh's head whipped in my direction, his eyes wide.

"Who dares–?" he stopped when he saw me. At his feet in the sand were a smattering of photocopied pages pocked wildly with symbols and strange words. He looked at the pages briefly before knocking them into the fire.

"*Dimitte me ut ignis, fac vindictam in me, et in nomine eius, gloria mea!*"

"I don't speak Latin," I said, pulling my .38 from my pocket and aiming for his chest.

He smiled. "You will die, nonethless," he said. He ripped open his shirt, exposing elaborate tattoos across his chest. "*Ignis!*" he said.

Flames engulfed his body. His still-living eyes locked on mine as he smiled again. With that, he turned and walked through the fire, moving towards the children.

I rounded the bonfire, putting myself between Raleigh and the children. I aimed the .38 for his face and squeezed the trigger.

A scorched skeleton collided with me, and my shot missed Raleigh. The creature, little more than a blackened torso, closed two hands around my throat as the burned skeleton's teeth began to chatter. *Clack clack clack clack clack clack–*

I slammed the butt of my pistol against the creature's skull, but the grip only tightened. Above me, Raleigh stalked past, eyes locked on the children, his burning lips repeating some forbidden incantation.

On the ground, the children's screams were muted beneath their gags.

A gunshot sliced through the night. Then a second. And a third.

Raleigh stumbled backwards as bullets slammed into his chest, his arms pinwheeling for balance.

A fourth shot passed through his head, spraying

blood into the air.

He collapsed on the sand beside me, dead.

As he died, all reanimated life in the skeleton ceased, its hands opened. I pushed the scorched torso off me and turned my eyes in the direction of the gunshot.

Sheriff Huggins was running towards us, gun raised. He holstered his pistol and knelt beside the children, his hands pulling at the ropes binding their hands.

"I got you," he said. "It's all right now, you're gonna be all right. I got you. I got you."

CHAPTER 28. THE
SALVATION STOMP

Gil was wearing a fleet of butterfly stitches across his forehead–they make him look tough, remember?–and was cutting a line across the dance floor like a madman. He'd slipped the DJ a twenty and was earning every penny dancing to T. Rex's "Bang a Gong."

It had been two days since our showdown with Fred Raleigh, his gang of Plague Doctors, and the missing FBI Black Ops agent. As luck would have it, Saturday night brought a fundraiser all-you-can-eat shrimp buffet/dance party at the local fire station, an event that Gil had demanded we attend.

Also in attendance were Clarissa and her new friends, the witches from Rehoboth's only coven, including Agatha and mean Myra. After hearing of what she'd done, the coven had accepted Clarissa with open arms. Finch looked equally bored and appalled, Willa was enjoying socializing with the townies, Gil was tearing up the dance floor, and I was tearing up the buffet. Before me sat a paper plate with a standing mountain of shrimp shells and two plastic cups with nothing left in them but beer foam. Finch sat across the table from me, watching the time on his watch, waiting for what Gil called the "polite departure time." Unfortunately for Finch, it was over an hour away.

"Have another beer," I said.

He looked at me like I'd suggested positively indecent. "It's *light* beer," he said. "That is... unacceptable. There is no wine, there is no gin, there is no scotch–"

I smiled. "Okay, okay."

A pair of what I guessed to be sun-aged widows were now flanking Gil, joining in his T. Rex infused bliss. It was hard not to feel good.

We'd beaten Raleigh and his skeleton docs–a good thing, freeing Clarissa and the children and putting an end to the strange rash of kidnappings the quiet seaside town had suffered. Sheriff Huggins had been thankful and gracious, if a little angry as to why we had not shared more information.

"Why didn't you tell me you were coming here?" he'd asked.

"It was... a hunch," I'd told him as the EMTs checked us out. "Just a hunch. How did you get here?"

"I checked on Raleigh's phone records and found that in addition to land lines and a cell, he paid a monthly bill for OnStar, that roadside assistance thing? I contacted them and they put a tracker on his truck that brought me to the Burton Island's visitor parking. From there, it wasn't hard to spot the fire."

"Not bad, Sheriff," I'd told him. "Not bad at all."

And it was true, for the amount of trouble we'd had with each other, he'd made good on his promise. He'd found the children, and without much help from me, either. He looked happy when, after the children were in the care of the EMTs, he'd helped his brother's widow into his cruiser and taken her safely home. Turns out Sheriff R. Lee Huggins was a good man, even if it took some time for me to learn that.

When the EMTs had given Jane the thumbs up, she'd said very little to me before disappearing into the night, not even waiting for a ride back to her cherry red BMW. She'd smiled, waved briefly, and said, "Give me a call sometime if you want to get another drink." And with that, she was gone. I didn't think twice about calling her. Knowing that she had a sense of responsibility assured me that she wasn't quite as bad as she wanted us to think she was.

Clarissa had made it all right. Other than a nasty shiner she'd gotten when Raleigh had kidnapped her, she'd gotten out of the whole ordeal relatively unscathed, and was now seen as a hero to boot. "My three kingfishers," she'd said when I'd helped Sheriff Huggins cut her bindings. "I knew it was a good omen when you came to town." I watched her speak with the other witches, a smile gracing her face for the first time in a long while.

Willa—aside from a hefty goose egg on her head— was fine. When she came to and found Jane gone, I am pretty sure she started feeling better already, although she would admit nothing. The next day, after our heads had cleared and we'd all gotten some food and sleep, she apologized.

"Things are complicated between you and I," she'd said. "I can't argue with that. And... I'm sorry if I put you in an awkward spot. Jane is... well, a better woman than I thought. I worry, but as long as you keep your head about you, I... I won't worry *too* much." She'd smiled sadly. "I don't have much right to worry, but anyway," she'd trailed off. "Sorry I was a bitch."

So... things were great. Right? I'd say so, three beers and about two dozen shrimp in, as I was. It was hard not to feel good in that situation. Gil kept dancing with his sun-baked widow friends–to "Take on Me" now–and I kept up with the shrimp and beer. Yes, things were good. I tried not to think about the still-missing *Red Dragon* grimoire, or the Black Ops FBI agent, or the tortured and murdered accomplice, or the Battery, or the idea that this was all leading towards something called *metempsychosis*: returning life to something lost to death. The Battery was enough trouble with their current line-up, I realized. Who knew what resources they had waiting on the bench, just itching to come back to life?

No, I didn't think about these things. What was the point?

This is the end of the story, isn't it?

CHAPTER 29. LIFE GOES ON

Not quite.

The "polite departure time" arrived, and Finch disappeared like a ghost at the stroke of midnight. I waited a few more minutes and slipped out, giving Willa a wave as I slipped out the doors. She smiled sadly as I did.

It was a beautiful evening, even better considering how our vacation had ended. I walked along the boardwalk, smelling the salt air, listening to the waves break on the beach, watching as the–

"Hey stranger," a voice called.

I turned towards a bench that overlooked the deserted beach. A man was seated on it, facing the ocean. He turned to face me, an understated smile on his face.

It was Carrion, dressed in a three piece pinstripe suit and smoking a long, fat cigar.

"Oh," I said.

He patted the bench at his side. "Why don't you have a seat?" he asked.

My mouth turned to cotton, and suddenly it seemed like my feet were attached to the boardwalk.

"Come on now, you're being indiscreet," Carrion said.

"Said the vampire in a three-piece suit at the beach," I muttered as I unstuck my feet and walked to him. He slid over, making more room for me, and I sat down.

The problem was, I never anticipated Greely to call Carrion. I'd just assumed that was all bluster. And yet, here he was. It was easy for me to be a mouthy hardass on the phone. It was a little harder for me to disobey authority in person.

"I... uh."

"It's all right," Carrion said, "you're not in trouble."

"Um, I'm–"

"Stop stuttering, Dylan," Carrion said, turning to face the ocean and blowing a plume of smoke into the air. "Relax and watch the sea, it's not good for me to get your blood pressure up. It's bad for business."

"Business?"

"You are an asset of mine," he reminded me. "I like you healthy. And happy."

I swallowed. "What are you doing here?"

"You probably imagine that I am here to scold you. Yes, I spoke with Greely, but I'm not mad. I don't like when assets push back, but in this case, it came quite in handy."

"How so?"

Carrion turned to face me for a second. "You think this was all us, don't you?"

"Wasn't it?"

"The kidnappings? The sloppy rituals? Gracious, no. Sacrificing children to raise the dead? How

263

gauche."

"If it wasn't you, who—"

"I can't answer questions of which I know not the answers," Carrion said.

"But the book. *The Red Dragon*—"

"*The Grand Grimoire*, please," Carrion said. "When you say *The Red Dragon*, you seem far too superstitious. You have to own what frightens you."

"What about it?" I asked. "You have it, don't you?"

He sighed. "We *had* it."

"Jane got it for you."

"Yes, she did."

"Why did you say 'had'?"

"Because that's the trouble with corporeal objects," Carrion said, tapping a flutter of cigar ash to the boardwalk, "they are so easy to steal."

"Someone stole it from you?"

He nodded.

"Who?"

"The same person behind your kidnappings, I would imagine."

I sat, thinking, trying to take those pesky loose ends and tie them up. The longer I sat, the calmer I got and the easier it was for my brain to work.

"Allagash," I said. "He's behind—"

"No," Carrion said. "Try again."

I thought for another moment. "Allagash works for you."

"Very good," Carrion said, patronizingly. "That's

what I like about you. You are very good at adding things up–if given enough tries to get it right."

I remember everything Willa had said about bank accounts. Our logic had been sound, I realized, we just weren't right about *everything*.

"That means you've been paying off the Mayor, too. And the City Manager?"

"Indeed I was. I very much needed to keep this quiet until I could get a contract to solve it for me. We at the Battery do not like our dirty laundry to be aired."

"Which is why the press didn't ever get in-volved," I said. "All right, then who was it?"

"I'm sorry?"

"Who did you have solve the problem for you?" I asked.

"Why, *you* of course. And I got you to do it for free."

I opened my mouth but couldn't find any words. When I'd signed up to work for the Battery, we'd agreed on seven contracts. Apparently, I'd just ful-filled one–*for free*.

"That's what Greely was calling about?" I asked.

"Yes, it was. So you see, that's why I said that I wasn't angry. You did me a favor, Dylan. For that, how could I be angry?"

I looked out at the ocean, a terribly hollow feeling filling my stomach, that feeling you get when you miss a *great* opportunity. In this case, two birds with one stone.

"Anyway, I just wanted to say thanks," Carrion

said, smiling. "And to let you know that, although you believe the Battery is the *only* villain game in town, it would seem someone else has purchased a seat at the table. And with *The Grand Grimoire* in their pocket, they should not be underestimated."

He stood, taking a long drag from his cigar and blowing a ring. "Enjoy what remains of your vacation," he said. "Rehoboth is such a delightful little town. Oh, and expect to hear again from Mr. Greely shortly. There is much for you to do," he said. "Much for you to do, indeed."

He turned away, and slowly, very slowly, he walked down the boardwalk into the night.

THE END

And this concludes *The Zeros and The Season of The Witch*. Further tales are already on their way. Visit www.GilsGrimoire.com for more information about upcoming adventures with Gil, Finch, Dylan, and their strange menagerie of friends.

The next Zeros novel, *The Zeros and The Empirical Evidence of Stars*, is coming soon. While you wait, satisfy your appetite by enjoying the first chapter of the upcoming novel!

CHAPTER 1. TROUBLE CALLS

The first time I got struck by lightning, I should have taken it as a portent of doom. As you can imagine, I didn't, and it was a mistake. So sue me, I'm new to this otherworld crap. The good news is that by the third time it happened, I'd figured out I was truly up shit creek.

It started outside a heavy oak door with Gil Abercrombie–my boss and weirdo demon fighter-cum-billionaire manchild extraordinaire (it's complicated)–on his hands and knees with one eye pressed to the less-than-generous crack between the carpet and the door. A pipe dangled from his lips, ash spilling free and soiling the carpet, foul smoke seeping up from the wooden bowl. Finch, his eternally youthful associate, stood behind him, scowling, hands crossed over his chest.

"And what do you see, Boss?"

"Same thing you saw, man, not a G.D. thing," Gil whispered through clenched teeth. "Are you sure she's here?"

"As I said, I don't believe she is. But no, I'm not certain," Finch said. "That's why we're... well, *peeking.*"

I shifted my weight and sighed for about the sixth

time. Gil ignored me; Finch's scowl worsened.

We were in a long beautiful hallway on the 19th floor of one of the few halfway decent condo complexes in Philadelphia. A plush oriental carpet ran the length of the beige hall, maybe thirty feet, from the window to our immediate left at the end of the hall to the bank of elevators at the opposite end. I think I was supposed to be the lookout, but in a straight corridor, there's not much looking out to be done. Thankfully, we had yet to see another tenant. Generally this kind of establishment, snooping is frowned upon. Even when you're a professional.

"Can you pick it?" Gil asked.

"I know a great many things," Finch whispered, leaning in close, "many of them unsavory, however, lock picking is not one of them, remember?"

"Yeah, I think our last foray into this territory of covert entrance proved I pretty much suck at it too," Gil mumbled. "Didn't I just kick the door in last time at that mansion? A good old heave-ho? I probably couldn't pick my way into a Fisher Price clubhouse. Not even one with one of those big red plastic toy locks. Although I can try when we get back to the office later."

There was a pause before both eyes turned to me.

"Aw, come on guys, don't make me do this," I pleaded.

"Shhhh, quiet, Dylan man. We're undercover here, remember? This is a big job and we really, *really* need this," Gil said.

"You know, I don't think any of that is true," I

said. "We're not even on a job."

"Well, it would be greatly appreciated," Finch said. "It would be the easiest way out of my current situation, and you know it would make the Boss incredibly happy. Now that I think about it, it would also help me avoid a rather sticky conversation with the condominium's board of directors."

"'Sticky conversation'? I thought this was all kosher."

"Don't even worry about it, chief," Gil interrupted, "you're a Special Forces superhero or whatever, just get all MacGyver on this thing and we'll be outta here before you know it. You can prolly pick this lock with a friggin' Popsicle. Really, Dylan man, it would make this so much easier. And it would be *so* badass."

I grumbled something. Then I grumbled some more. I'd only been doing this for a few months, and even though I'd been hired as the driver and heavy lifter, I'd gotten used to being the human Swiss Army knife. Finally, I said, "All right, what do you have on you? I'll need a pick and a tension wrench. Small and thin and strong."

Finch and Gil patted down their pockets. Finch looked at me and shrugged; empty-handed. Gil handed me a broken half of a pencil.

"Are you serious?" I asked.

Gil squirmed sheepishly. A flash of lightning broke through the autumn sky, sending our long shadows stretching down the hall for a moment. Gil and Finch turned to look out over the city, distracted. Outside the window at the end of the hall, we could see the four masts of the docked Moshulu rising and falling on the storm-stirred tide of the Delaware. I leaned in between them and pounded on the door with my balled fist.

Finch sighed, perpetually nonplussed. Gil raised a finger to his lips and let loose a ferocious *"SHHHHHHHHHHH!"*

"Sorry, guys," I shrugged.

Gil, eyes wide and mouth hanging agape, begged, "What did you *do*??"

From behind the door, I heard the tapping of heels on hardwood floor as footsteps moved from the interior of the condo towards us. They were rapid and heavy with determination. "She's *here*," Gil moaned as he scrambled to his feet and made to run away. Before he could make it two feet, Finch clamped a hand to his elbow.

"Oh, no you don't," Finch said, frowning. "This was your idea. You wanted her out of your apartment…"

The door opened.

A woman stood before me, long blonde hair falling down onto her tanned bare shoulders, a look of indescribable rage plastered across her face, but even the rage couldn't mask her beauty. Super-model thin and above-average height, she wore long skin-tight jeans and what would charitably be described as a tank top, although it was probably just a pair of napkins suspended by strands of dental floss. I made a conscious decision to keep my eyes directed north of her chin for fear of what they might see otherwise. She couldn't have been more than twenty-two and I felt like a dirty old man just standing in front of her. To be frank, I don't think I *really* knew what buxom meant until that very moment. I cleared my throat and checked my watch as to look busy. I wasn't wearing one.

"Finchy," she said, fixing her rapier eyes on Finch's pale face. "And Gilly. My *boys*. What a truly wonderful surprise to see you." She stepped into the hall on stilettos and slipped her arm through Finch's, pulling him inside. As she approached, I felt myself engulfed by the heavy effluvium of terribly sweet perfume. "Come in, come in, come in," she said. The rage had disappeared from her face, an arrogant gleam of smugness had taken its place. "You've been *avoiding* my calls, Finchy," she said with a hurt frown.

She closed the door behind me, Finch still tethered to her arm. "And who is this big hunk of man?" She asked, her hazel eyes moving the sizable distance upward to my own.

"Uh, er," I choked on a few more syllables before perhaps bubbling out, "Dylan… um, mhmm."

"*Dylan*," she said, smiling as the words escaped her red lipsticked lips. "It's a pleasure to meet you." She extended her bronzed hand to me and shook mine gently. "I'm Lizzy."

Finch coughed, a touch of color returning to his ghost-like face. "Elizabeth, I came here to speak with you. I –"

"There's plenty of time for talk later, Finchy," she said, leading us all deeper into the condo and depositing us onto a pair of couches that sat facing each other. I was next to Gil. She still stood sentinel with Finch attached to her arm. "Y'all want a drink?" she asked sweetly.

Gil nodded dumbly. I probably did, too.

She led Finch out of the room, supposedly towards the kitchen. As soon as they were gone, I turned to Gil, suddenly understanding the desperation.

"What the hell *is* she? A siren? A succubus? A nymph? A water sprite? A harpy? Lamia reincarnate?" I'd been diligent in my new otherworld education, having only scant months to make up for countless years of missing experience. "My god, man, what *is* she?"

"A waitress," Gil mumbled, his eyes closed and his head shaking slowly. "She got those chops at Hooters. It ain't natural, man."

"*What*?"

"Other than waitressing and wielding some faux southern hospitality, I don't even want to *think* about what else she's good at," he said, shaking his head again. "Gross."

"What are we *doing* here?"

"Trying to save Finch," Gil said, finally opening his eyes again. "He's been all... weird and stuff recently."

"So she *is* a succubus or something? I knew it. You can tell," I mumbled. "It's those eyes."

"A succubus? Only in the 'Men are from Venus' sense, I guess. Or... who sang that song 'Man Eater'? Hall and Oates?"

"Oh, boy," I said.

"This is the third time I've tried to get him to

break up with her. She's high maintenance and irrational and hyper-emotional, not to mention certifiably bananas crazy. The problem is that every time I convince him and he goes to do it, he comes back to the penthouse with a hickey on his neck and a sheepish look on his face. Somehow she's been convincing him to stay. So this time we came with him - you know, moral support - to get my copy of the deed to this place so he could just get the landlord to throw her skinny ass out of here. Plan was we were gonna sneak in, grab it, and skedaddle. It woulda worked until you *knocked* on the damn door."

"Well Finch doesn't seem to mind so much."

"What do you mean? He's acting even more brain-drained than usual. She's got all this pink shit and she's always playing with her hair and kissing him and stuff. She's terrible, man."

"But what's the deal? Magic? Brainwashing?"

Gil cleared his throat and blushed. "I'd rather not speculate on her particular, eh, *brand* of persuasion."

Sharp heel taps on the wood floor signaled the happy couple's return. Lizzy was liberally reapplying red lipstick while Finch–blushing, disheveled, and neatly stenciled set of a red lips on his cheek–carried a small tray with three glasses on it.

"I figured a drink would be nice for y'all," she said, directing the glasses from the tray into our hands like a symphony conductor. After a moment, she took a seat on the couch across from us, her arm slipping through Finch's as he took his place beside her.

I took a gulp. "Thank you."

If my drink was big, Gil's was huge. He tipped

what must've been a pint glass back and downed a third of the drink, grimacing as he did. He didn't drink much. When he was done, he took a deep breath. "So. How are you doing, Lizzy?"

"Oh, I'm fine, Gil, just fine. I been waitin for you and Finchy to swing by and see how I'm doing. You've been keeping my man busy here at work, I guess." The last sentence had a definite ring of bitterness coursing through it.

"Well, uh, yeah, we been pretty busy, I figure. Ain't that right, Dylan?"

I nodded, doing what little I could to stay out of it.

"How long you been workin with these two, Mr. Dylan?" Lizzy asked, batting her eyelashes in my direction.

"A few months," I said, shifting my drink between hands. "I started with them early in the summer."

"Ain't that something," she said, leaning forward, somehow managing to lower her already plunging neckline. "What kind of work do you do for these two?"

"Umm…"

"Finchy here tells me that you guys are some kind of financial consultants? Something about contracting out to banks all over the country?"

I looked at Finch beside Liz. His eyes widened as he shrugged almost imperceptibly. I cleared my throat and smiled. "I'm just the driver," I said. "But that's right, independent financial and communication consultants."

She smiled, showing off teeth white enough to burn retinas. "That sounds mighty exciting."

"Oh yeah, it has its rewards. And *drawbacks*." I kicked Gil's foot under the table.

"Well, isn't that somethin," she said, turning to Finch and smiling. "So what brings y'all out here tonight?"

Gil coughed dramatically and sat forward, leaving his now nearly empty glass on a small coffee table. "I think, uh, Finchy has something he wants to say to you."

Liz turned to Finch, her look troubled. "What is it sugarpie baby doll? You all right?"

I groaned. I couldn't help it. Pet names will do that to me.

"Well..." Finch turned over a few broken syllables. She looked concerned and rubbed one hand up and down his thigh. I had to give it to her, she had something going for her.

"Remember?" Gil said, all but reaching across the table and nudging Finch with his elbow. "What we talked about this afternoon over ribs and beans?" His hands started moving in senseless pantomimes. "About... *you know*." The last bit was stage-whispered as if Liz was not sitting just beside Finch.

Finch nodded, his uncharacteristic flush beginning to dissipate. "Elizabeth, I must talk to you about..." he swallowed, marshaling some momentum. "About the future. About where this is going."

A dark cloud seemed to be forming over Liz's

head, a slight line appearing on her otherwise perfect brow. "Finchy, what are you on about?"

It didn't take Dr. Phil or a sideshow psychic to see that she knew where this was heading. I didn't care *too* much, but it did feel a little like we were ambushing her, and I guess we were. She may have been a normal run of the mill quasi-succubus, but I still felt bad for her. Her end was nigh. I kept up the squirming.

"Well, I've been wanting more space recently, and it's gotten me to thinking about what I want versus, well, versus what you want." Finch glanced at Gil, who was nodding enthusiastically.

"Uh huh," Liz said.

A rumble of thunder rolled through the room followed by a distant flash of lightning that poured light in through the wide windows behind Gil and me.

"And I, well, I think that…"

"Go on," Gil muttered under his breath.

"…I think that…"

"…just say it…"

"…I think it's time-"

The phone rang, a loud chiming of a digital bell somewhere near the kitchen. My eye followed the noise to a novelty telephone shaped like a pair of red lips. Seemed about right.

"You hold that thought, Finchy," Liz said, patting his arm before standing in a hurry. Her stilletos clacked across the hardwoods to the phone.

That's when I felt it: a change in the pressures and electrical consistencies of the room, like someone had just plugged a 1000 watt hairdryer into the wall and dropped it into a bathtub. Like I said: over the past few months, I'd been studying and training tirelessly, doing whatever I could to learn a little bit more about the *other* elements, the powers and forces that lay just beyond our normal everyday world. Yeah, I was still a neophyte, but I'd been able to expand on my meager five senses to a respectable ten or eleven as my body grew and changed, expanding under the tutelage of otherworld physiology in the form of a vael–a sentient injection of high-octane supernatural power that had forever changed who I was and what I was capable of. I'd picked it up accidentally after an unfortunate run-in with a Djinn during my early days with the gang. At first, it was weird, but I was getting used to being a hot-rodded guy with superhuman abilities, abilities I was *some-times* able to control. Gil and Finch kept telling me how "lucky" I was that the vael chose me as its host, seeing as how I was now capable of feats even they could only dream of. Me, I was reserving judgment on the thing.

"Liz, wait." I turned to Gil, "Do you feel that?" The hairs on my arms stood on end and I felt a static tingling move from my elbows down to my fingertips.

Gil turned to me, frowning and sputtering. "Dammit man, he was so *close*! He was really gonna do it that time! You know how long it takes to convince him to do anything? I could feel the ax falling!"

"No, Gil, something else. Something's wrong. Do you feel that?"

"Hush up now boys and hold your horses, this'll

just take a minute," Liz said as she leaned in to lift the receiver.

"Wait," I said, "No wait, stop!" I stood and slipped past Gil, moving towards Liz as the first drops of rain began to patter against the wide windows to my right. "Liz, don't pick up that–"

She lifted the receiver, or in this case, the top lip of the big red plastic pair.

"Stop!" I shouted as an explosive crash of thunder made the floor beneath my feet shake.

Above us, the light bulb encased in a blown glass globe exploded, as did the bulbs mounted in sconces along the living room wall and one on a table lamp standing beside Gil. Liz gasped as the room was plunged into darkness.

"What the hell?" Gil said, rising to his feet.

"Elizabeth," Finch said, his voice stern and replete with the harsh logic that I'd come to expect from him. "Dylan is right, put the phone down. Put it down *now*."

Liz stood in the dim light from the city skyline outside to my left, the phone hanging in her hand, her mouth gaping slightly, a look of shock on her face. "What's going on?" she whispered. "What're ya'll –"

She was five paces away. I reached out to her. "Liz, give me the–"

The bolt of lightning came like a howitzer, blowing out the glass like confetti and hitting me like a battering ram just below my right collarbone. It was a twisted ray of unimaginable light and heat. When it hit me, everything turned white for a moment as my body was lifted from the ground and launched backwards. I remember crashing into the living room's far wall and feeling the crunch of glass and wood against my spine. I fell to the floor in a storm of crushed picture frames and drywall fragments.

I heard Liz screaming and the rush of feet as Finch and Gil ran towards me. It was hard to open my eyes. It felt like my eye lashes had burned together, and they probably had. They made a crinkling sound when I pulled them apart. Everything was blurry at first, Gil and Finch stood crouched on either side of me. Liz kept screaming.

As things came back into focus, I saw Liz, standing at the opposite side of the room, horrified, eyes wide, phone receiver still dangling from her hand. I took a deep breath and tried to speak, but I couldn't make a sound.

"Don't talk," Finch said.

"You all right? Hey big man," Gil tapped my cheeks with his open hands. "Come on, buddy, can you hear me? Dylan?"

I extended my index finger in Liz's direction and struggled to lift my arm, but it felt like an anvil. It was just too heavy, or I was just too weak. I sighed, the only sound I could muster.

When the second flash of light appeared, I assumed I was dead. But I wasn't, not yet. Tiny cerulean bolts of light jumped from the mouthpiece on the receiver and forked, lancing like two prongs of a fork straight into Liz's chest. Her eyes splayed open and I heard the sharp intake of breath as her body convulsed momentarily before the light was gone. Gil and Finch turned to face her only when they heard the clatter of the receiver falling to the hardwood floor.

"What're you doin, girl? Call for help!" Gil shouted. "The rescue squad!"

Finch's eyes dwelled on her a moment longer before he turned back to me, a mix of fear and confusion on his face. He met my eyes and I tried to nod. Gil stayed at my side as Finch rose to attend to Liz, her body slumping against the nearby table for support.

I closed my eyes again and began slipping out of consciousness. The last time I opened them, I remember seeing smoke and I thought, *what's that burning smell?*

It took me a moment to realize it was me.

ABOUT THE AUTHOR

Eric Bonkowski lives in Delaware. He is inspired daily by Saturday afternoon cliffhanger serials, classic comics and comic strips, and horror films of the '30s and '40s–to say nothing of mystery, fantasy, and science fiction pulp writings of every age.

He spends his time reading, watching campy movies, and writing, supported all the while by his remarkable wife and family. During the rare quieter moments, he can be found listening to jazz and falling asleep well before bedtime.

He is the author of the *Gil's Grimoire* series and the *Brick Brannigan* series.

Visit him at:

http://www.GilsGrimoire.com

http://www.BrickBrannigan.com

www.ingramcontent.com/pod-product-compliance
Lightning Source LLC
Chambersburg PA
CBHW020238180626
46810CB00006B/2262